THE GOLDEN AGE: ORDER OF THE GOLDEN DAWN

Aly Maredia

THE GOLDEN AGE: ORDER OF THE GOLDEN DAWN

Vanguard Press

VANGUARD PAPERBACK

A CIP catalogue record for this title is
available from the British Library.

ISBN 978 1 784658 45 8

Vanguard Press is an imprint of
Pegasus Elliot MacKenzie Publishers Ltd.
www.pegasuspublishers.com

First Published in 2020

Vanguard Press
Sheraton House Castle Park
Cambridge England

Printed & Bound in Great Britain

Dedication

To an incredibly supportive family, and friends (you know your names) and the editorial team gracious enough to bring this work to life.

Acknowledgements

As mentioned previously, this first work has only been made possible by a team of several people, edging me an inch (or a centimetre, depending on what you prefer) at a time, and an inspiration from the ensnaring *Skulduggery Pleasant* books by Derek Landy, without which this idea wouldn't have been sparked during my teenage years. My supportive team involves my parents and maternal family. It'd to fair to say that they're the best people in the world from my point of view. And friends – Wilco and Lewis and Karl, and other RuneScape friends – people whom I met online but helped me tremendously with snippets of research, and of course, reminding me that I actually had to write besides just promising that I had something going on. Jeremy and Nikolina, for sticking by no matter what. And last but not the least, my once best friend on whom Maverick is based – you legend.

Prologue

Year 2030, August 17, Aaron B.

The sky is hellish red, with the last tinge of twilight barely breaking through. It is like the bloodshed from war, splattered across the sky. Or perhaps it just represents the inner manifestation of my state. Either way, it is bone-chilling cold in this shelter, in the midst of August. Who would've thought that? The nuclear winter seems like it will engulf us all forever. It will be the Mankind's winter, caused by the world war. No life, no warmth, just overcast sky and dying crops.

The water is irradiated, so I had to travel three hundred miles inland just to reopen our old shelter. I only imagine that our troops, by far, have been lost. Yet, I could not but enjoy soaking in the warmth of uncontaminated water. I hated to leave them… but it had to be done. I have to move on to the next thing. I dread to put so much behind, yet I must muster the courage to do whatever it takes. The next thing is of much greater weight to carry. As the founder of the resistance.

I wouldn't dream once in a millennia that we'd inspire citizens and armies around the entire world to stand up together against the elites and their single, all-powerful government, which they refer to as the Sanctum. This is the beginning of their New World Order. If we accept defeat, this small group will then control the history and the tides of human future.

At least, it united the people. The prospect of people unequivocally fighting an all-powerful enemy came true, too, like from some legend.

But… we've almost lost. The East European resistances have crumbled like dust.

The Russian resistance has accepted bitter defeat and has been exiled in a newly formed state called Scythe, where the rebels can hide. I couldn't get in contact with anyone in Middle East and India. They're like a nuclear black hole now. We are the last resistance fighting for freedom in the US.

Meanwhile, the Sanctum has started the implementation of the tracking chip to take control of the civilians by surgically implanting it in their napes. If this process keeps spreading globally, no man will have free will ever again.

Yet, this is not the end. I have found what I had to. I have found this **rift** they are after — the source of all Powers, seeping from another dimension. The powers which can make us into…

Suddenly, the man was startled to his feet, spilling the ink pod across the table, as the radio burst in static and came to life.

"This is to inform the states of Texas, Alabama... at 7pm approximately..." and the voice broke into further static with a screech. The man got up, trying to tune the radio. "To have their provisions and seek nearby fallout shelters"; and then the radio went out again.

He didn't try to tune in again. He didn't have to. He knew dreadfully well what the broadcast meant. The cities which were riling up with chaos and civil war due to the bulk of armed resistances were going to be nuked. In how much time? He didn't know. He started pacing. His fingers twitched anxiously. Someone should've reached out to him by now, but they hadn't. He paced faster. The clock ticked. He looked at it: quarter until seven.

Fifteen minutes, he thought... a blink of time, in reality, before the strike. He always viewed reality in blinks. A small event which momentarily seemed to be endless, or a phase of life lasting for years, all seemed like a blink upon passing.

This blink was different, though. This was the last blink for him. He never cared about dying, yet something about first-hand nuclear death chilled him to the marrow. He felt his bowels turning. The nuclear telecasts had always haunted him as a child, even when nothing else in particular ever scared him. Something about it seemed so absurd and almost unreal. It gave mankind a godly power, a power to doom the very planet which gave birth to it.

The windows rattled as a car screeched to a halt. Help had arrived; perhaps he could escape the blast radius. He glanced at the clock: two minutes to seven. Any gladness he felt paled immediately.

The door burst open as the doctor rushed in. He looked around until his eyes landed on the man. He then rushed and grabbed both of the man's arms, his eyes frantic and searching for an answer.

"Brother, we must do something!"

"What? We can't go anywhere now. We can hide in the basement… but then our car will be gone. Who knows how long until it would be safe enough to come out in the fallout? And then there's if we have any food in the basement at all."

The doctor shook his head, his eyes still frantic, even though his breathing had levelled. He was always a little different to anyone else.

"No. We left this place because it was haunted… it haunts now, too. Down there is where most people were turned into corpses."

"Then clearly we can't stay and accept our fate." The man broke free and walked towards the window; the sky was now completely blood red.

"Do you see that? The fate shows us that we will be just another two drops of blood in the sky." His hand twitched, his soul screamed to shove his brother into the basement, but he couldn't. He didn't want his brother to go through that trauma all over again. Yet, his hesitation was inevitably going to cause his brother's death. Overthinking really was the habit which would follow him to his grave. He looked up again: only a minute to go.

"Brother. No poetic ending today. The world becomes more haunted by the second. The Sanctum has opened the rift," said the doctor.

The man swung around, with a brief expression of horror, before it turned into rage. "You're telling me that their lunatic leader discovered a way to access this rift before us?"

"Yes, and they mean to use it. If they truly are able to establish a force of supernaturally powerful men, then humanity will forever be enslaved."

"God dammit… Well, then, our solace is that at least our research would work."

"It would work, yes, but only if we had more time."

And then they looked up again: it was already a couple of minutes past seven. They didn't have to wait. They didn't feel shocked when the ground shuddered beneath them with the initial shockwave of the explosion. The man took his fragile brother under his embrace, and looked at the beautiful horizon one last time before closing his eyes.

A misty window

Jack woke up with a start, having nodded off for the third time. In his hand, he still held the cup with swirling milk tea which had now gone cold. He sighed, feeling its coldness. Even with the heating, the office was chilled. The cubicles in either direction, were all empty. Of course, they would be. It was a week before the parade festival, celebrated around the world at the end of each century in honour of Paragon, the ruler of the Sanctum.

It was the dawn of the twenty-sixth century, four hundred years after World War Three. It was thought to be the end of humanity then. No one knew how, but it was considered an absolute truth that the Sanctum had saved them. Each working day started with the pledge to the Sanctum.

Jack heard the usual oaths from the office speakers, and the morning news telecast. He clutched the paper in his hand, with dried-up ink spilled across it. He was beyond surprised for what he had read. For the first time ever, he had read about the war from the perspective of the people blamed for causing World War Three.

Being a child who grew up in the current world, he knew no better. In fact, not so long ago everything would have seemed mundane to him, but it was as if he woke up one morning and felt snapped out of his reality. He was curious about the history which was lost during the war due to its scale — but whatever it was besides the page from this diary — it was gone. Jack was growing skeptical in a world where no-one would ever understand his paranoia.

But the page wasn't the only thing concerning him. He could've been enjoying the holidays much like the public, but something had caught his attention. The murder case which he was working on was, for some reason, declared confidential and discarded by the higher-ups.

Something really did not seem right to him. Why would they do that? There werc virtually almost zero crimes which went unpunished in this world, so why now would they hide it? With his impulses getting the better of him, he decided to call Mr Beck, the overseer of the entire Information Regulation department. In truth, Mr Beck was in a much too high a position to be contacted by an office worker like Jack. But, being a person of curious nature, and humble behaviour, he would often talk with individual employees on his rare visits. And, not so long ago, he shared his contact information with Jack because he found him impressive.

"Hello… Ah, good morning, Jack."

"Oh. Hi… yeah, I am Jack," Jack stammered, surprised that Mr Beck would have remembered him.

He was met with a soothing chuckle. "I would hardly exchange my contact details unless there is something to remember. But, you know, I could always pretend to remember you, as my occupation would allow."

They both chuckled, with Jack sheepishly realising that he wasn't making a great impression. "Apologies, Mr Beck. I know it is not appropriate to call in the festive period, but I happened to be working on…"

"The case? The mysterious death of Allen, a farmer from Kansas?"

"Yes. I have never seen such cases going unsolved, yet this possible murder was restricted from further investigation. Why?"

"I do not know, Jack. I was concerned just like you. My position does hold some power and charm, but I am just a middleman, nonetheless. Sanctum does not give us information if it considers it unnecessary to be disclosed to the public."

Jack sighed, clenching his jaw, wondering what other outcome had he expected in the first place? "It is okay, Mr Beck. Thank you."

"Ah, feisty young man, don't be disappointed. I sense the passion which has brought you thus far at such a young age. I remember when my bones were just as fiery when it came to things. These days, unfortunately, they barely crackle in the winter."

Despite his disappointment, Jack laughed as the call ended. With a voice as serene as that, he could hardly be mad at Mr Beck. At least he understood why it was bothering Jack, while others looked on him as crazy and just asked him to trust the Sanctum.

Jack sighed and swung his chair around, looking through the glass wall of the office. The view directly overlooked Central Park, New York. A view which he was so pleasantly eager to see every day was nothing but a solemn smudge through the frost-covered window panes. Jack didn't know what it was, but he did not feel the joy which every single person seemed to be having for the parade. They would get to see Paragon, the Holy Knights, and a magnificent show of powers that only happened once a century. Yet, he felt empty and disconnected.

He felt the texture of the ancient paper once again in his hand, feeling how delicate it was. Feeling chills, wondering what happened to the man who had stopped him from writing. What was that discovery he spoke of? Was it possible that he had an explanation for the powers which the people of Sanctum had? Not today, he thought. Whatever it was, today was not the day he was going to worry about these things.

The evening felt great after not having a break for as long as he could remember. He was mesmerised by the renovation of the pub after not having visited it for a year. It was completely changed, as if its owner and the bartender, Brock, had just bought a completely new place.

Glancing around, he saw the place had been redone with dark wooden furniture, which he presumed to be made of mahogany. Complete with varnished floor and the walls panelled in intricately carved wood, depicting the symbols of the Sanctum and the silhouettes of the knights. The roof itself was a screen depicting a starry night with snowflakes drifting down, as if to emulate the spirit of festivity. Jack was not savvy at all when it came to such things, but 'expensive' was all that he could think of.

The place brimmed with people and their festive aura. Jack sat at a table near the bar, the same as where they always sat. He tapped his fingers anxiously, waiting for his best friend Alexander to arrive.

It is going to be like a blink, he thought to himself, reflecting on Aaron's depiction of the passing of time. However, before he could drift off in his own thoughts, he saw his friend. Tall and lean, clad in a white V-necked shirt. His unmistakable blue eyes sparkled and his dazzling grin dulled almost everyone else in the room. He sauntered towards the table, with his golden locks flowing at either side of his brows.

The bartender, Brock, beamed and waved at them when he saw them together. He seemed lively and full of zest, which was hardly surprising. Jack still remembered when Brock had required his financial help, but he was way beyond even him now.

"Long time no see, eh?" Brock exclaimed, slamming three pints of ale on the table and slumping down on one of the chairs. He had become stockier since Jack last remembered.

"All I know is you're doing well and I am not," Jack quipped.

"Well, good time, good days, man. Now cheer up, you miser," said Brock, gulping down the foaming ale.

So did two of the boys; Alex rushed to finish his pint before Brock, but ended up spilling it on his shirt. "Ah, Paragon damn this," he said, flushing up.

"Ha, ha, ha! And you are supposed to be in the military or something?" Brock exhaled, passing him a napkin.

"Yeah, whatever. At least my chair doesn't wail when I sit."

Brock was mildly scorned at the jibe. "Anyhow, how did your overseas service go? Get to see anything related to the parade?"

"Ah, right, actually you guys won't believe what I saw there."

Both the men were immediately drawn in.

"So, you know, how I am a novice soldier only? Typically, you need five years of training to be even deployed as a Sanctum foot soldier, before we take the oath and get our cool exoskeleton suits. Well, this year they actually called all the novices to help with the logistics of setting up the parade in all major cities."

"So, did you see anything?" Jack whispered.

"No, I'd be lucky to see a bear crap in the woods where I was stationed."

Both the men erupted into laughter. Brock patted his shoulder in mock consolation.

"What about you then, big man? Not bad at all with what you did with this place," Alex said, having a long, curious glance of the surroundings.

"Well, pretty good, as you can see. I have been doing some side business as well."

"Like what? Selling more ale?"

"Eh, I'd rather keep that to myself."

"All right, suit yourself. What about you, Jack; how have you been doing?"

Jack flinched, having been idle for most of the conversation. Alex pleasantly smiled towards him as usual. "Well, for the most part," he said, rubbing the sleep from his eyes, "I received this murder case a couple of weeks back. Before our department could forward it for regular news broadcasting, the Sanctum informed us that it had been declared confidential and was meant to be trashed."

"Could you tell us anything about the case? Or the chip number of the victim?" Brock inquired. By chip number, he meant that every citizen, besides their name, could be looked up on a database called the Common Registry, using the number of the tracking chip implanted in their nape upon birth. It was unique to each individual.

"You know we cannot ask that, right?" Alex intervened. "The Sanctum has officially declared it confidential."

"Simmer down, young man. It's not a big deal."

Alex frowned towards Jack, as if asking whether Brock was going too far.

"It's all right. I don't care about it all that much," shrugged Jack.

"Well then, I would rather not be involved in this as a supposed-to-be soldier and all. You guys, do you?" said Alex curtly, and briskly walked out of the pub after shaking their hands.

"It's all right, Jack," Brock reassured him, looking at Jack's disappointment. "It seems to me you… are not like him any more. You are not like them. You know."

"What do you mean?" Jack spluttered in surprise.

"You very well know the world isn't as normal as it seems, or as peaceful. There is something roiling beneath the peace of this very festivity. There is something… not right."

Jack swallowed. He had no idea whether Brock was being facetious or he somehow knew about what Jack had been up to. How Jack felt these days could well be considered a crime for questioning the Sanctum.

"Brock, uh, I have to go."

"Where? It's still early. Offices are closed from tomorrow until the new year."

"I mean, I don't know… the same place where Alex went," said Jack, and walked out of the pub, flushing at his own stupid response.

Alley of remorse

The alleyway behind Brock's pub was dark, lit only barely by the lamp-post on the sidewalk. Occasionally, a couple of cars passed by, but none paid attention to the ordeal within the alley.

"We told you not to do it!" grunted a balding man in a very raspy voice, and a strange accent very much unheard of. "But you had to." He choked Brock against the wall as his spittle smothered Brock's face.

"Gah, that's enough. Your mouth's been reeking like a dead rat," said another man, stepping into view, wearing a black, wide-brimmed hat and a black overcoat.

"Well, boy, that's how interrogation's done. Back in my day we'd beat 'em bloody — unlike now."

The man in the overcoat chuckled despite himself, but it went as quick as it came. "Well then, Brock. You know what you were told to do?"

"Yes."

"Why, then… why did you go around busting your mouth in front of him?"

"I- I don't know. I just thought he should know the truth…"

"Oh, really? And what's with this outrageous circus you've made of the pub? Clearly there can't be a noble reason for attracting attention?"

Brock was the on the edge of hyperventilating at this point. "I, uh… my renovation has symbols about our world — the people deserve to know that, too."

The man made an impatient grunt that sounded equal to part disappointment.

"Whatcha think we should do with this idiot?" asked the raspy-voiced, bald man to him.

"Eh, I don't know; he's of no use now. If he hadn't screwed up the conversation, we'd have enough time to kidnap him."

"He only left a couple of minutes ago," Brock whimpered desperately, knowing well where this was all going.

Wordlessly, the man in the overcoat jumped and elbowed Brock in the throat, pinning him to the wall and squashing him instantly. His body slumped over to the ground, but he was still alive enough to wheeze. The man then raised his hand and snapped down his open palm, instantly crushing Brock's throat with a field of invisible ripples and killing him.

"We'll take the body with us, so none of this has ever happened."

"And what about him? How do we get him now?"

"We'll get him. We will get Jack the old-fashioned way."

Music drifted from somewhere across the alley. It was a feminine voice, being a mumble under some strange, eccentric music, very much like the situation. Brock's murderer realised that they weren't the only presence in this alley. A figure in an overcoat just like him, his hair swept across his brows, and with prominent, sad-looking grey eyes, stood watching at the entrance. This was the man they were looking for; but before he could act, the witness across the alley bolted for his dear life.

One-way fantastical escapade

The ceiling withstood its image with the passing of time, a pentagonal shape painted blue, with a white, triangular medallion in between. There was a small circular light etched into the centre of the medallion.

Jack woke up some time ago, not knowing how much time had passed since he passed out. His eyes felt strained from dried-up tears. The sleep itself wasn't mellow, either. It took him right back to the scene. Brock slouched against the wall, the lifeless face. Just hours ago, he saw him bellowing... and then just his dead face. It was unreal.

He tried to remember the face of Allen the farmer, who was the victim of the murder case which Jack was investigating. He didn't remember much, besides staying at his farm in Kansas as a child, and the golden wheat fields, near a countryside road. He supposedly took care of Jack for some time as a relative when his parents left him there for a reason he didn't remember. That was until the Sanctum orphanage took him away as a toddler.

He heard a gentle knock on the door. It was probably Milly, an office colleague and manager of the apartment complex provided by their department. He snapped his fingers, and the automated door clicked open.

"Is everything all right?"

Jack gave a cursory nod, rubbing the sleep away from his eyes.

"So," he said, before pausing. "You received any information from the authorities?"

Milly nodded, pursing her lip, her deep green eyes filled with uncertainty. "Well, they told me to quickly move you out of this place, as there's a threat to your safety and the rest of the staff residing in this complex."

Jack looked up, startled. "Why?"

"Well, after your friend's murder… I mean, I am sorry, but it isn't safe here any more; you will have to leave. That is what I have been told."

"Only for me? Not you? The rest of the staff in this building?"

"No."

"Well then, I am staying."

"Why? You have to…"

"I am not going anywhere. Not until I find what all this mysterious fuss is and who those guys were."

Milly walked up to him and placed a hand on his shoulder. "I am sorry, Jack, but we have to leave it to the Paragon sometimes. I know you must feel the guilt, but sometimes we must leave it to the higher power."

"WHAT HIGHER POWER?" he yelled. "The one that is letting innocent people die?"

Milly pulled her hand back in surprise.

"This is it, Jack. We're doing this for your own safety, and if you do not comply, I will have to call security."

Before the conversation escalated further, the ground thrummed. First faintly, and then violently, and then it was as if, somewhere, the walls were being torn apart.

The noise of gunshots and the buzz from the discharge of rifles grew closer by the second.

"Come, we have no time!" Milly grabbed his hand and yanked him out of bed. It didn't take long for the surrounding situation to kick in for Jack. She ran as fast as she could, and he followed.

Out in the hall, they could already hear the fight getting closer at an astronomical rate.

They charged to their right — the only way they could have run — and away from the fight. They took a sharp left, and into a corridor with empty apartments on either side.

"Can someone explain why this is happening, and why we are running?" Jack asked, running ahead of Milly.

"To save our lives," gasped Milly, frantically turning a corner and then stopping.

"We can stay here for a moment, I guess," she said, still gasping for breath. "Why aren't you bothered whatsoever?" She appeared embarrassed by her exhaustion, while Jack barely broke a sweat.

"Well, I exercise."

"Well, that's funny for a recluse. Who would've thought you ever left your room?" she said, and started charging again.

"I actually get out of my home often."

"Like when?"

"Uh, none of your business."

Milly smiled at his retort, but they were sprinting too fast once again to speak.

They stopped again moments later, trying to guess which direction to run in, but they hesitated when the ground shook beneath them, and the solidness of the floor turned into air. The floor passed his eyes, but he grabbed a protruding cable from the broken ground just in time. He felt a pair of hands holding onto his legs as he was about to yell for Milly.

"Paragon, save us!" she screamed.

"Actually, the only thing saving you right now is me and my right arm, and it's about to be ripped from its socket. Now climb up..." Jack clenched his jaw, thinking for a moment. "Wait! I will swing myself a little and grab a cable with my other arm, and then you climb over me."

Milly did as she was told. It took the life out of her to pull herself up to his knees, and then she held on as tightly as she could.

"Okay, then. Hold tight." He tried to shift his balance and swung to bring his left arm up and grab the cable. The momentum was too much; he grunted and came down again, but this time he slipped down a notch. His hand was getting numb and the blood was trickling. He tried once again with all his strength, this time only barely managing to grab onto a cable with his left arm.

"Okay, climb." He gritted his teeth so tight that they could break.

"Uh? How? I…"

"CLIMB OVER ME!" he half screamed and half grunted. Realisation dawned in her deep, sea green eyes and she started climbing. As soon as she was up, she thrust out both of her hands for Jack to hold.

"Thanks," he said, but started pulling himself up.

Buzz.

And then he felt his right arm go completely numb. He slipped, hanging with one arm only.

"What was that?" Milly screamed, struck by the shock.

Jack looked across the corridor where he was hanging. There was an armed militant, clad in blue combat vest and deep green combat suit. He had a lightning-discharge rifle taken from a Sanctum soldier.

The man almost raised his rifle again, but the wall beside him blew, and a soldier burst through.

"They want me," Jack said, looking up at Milly. "You go."

"Wait; how do you know? He just shot you!"

"He did, but only to stop me from pulling up…"

"Stop it, and get up!"

She grabbed his left arm with both her hands and pulled as hard as she could. Although, for a moment, it did seem like he was being hoisted up, she failed to pull and he went back to a dead hang. She tried again, but slipped and fell on her butt.

Below, the militant across the corridor raised his hand and then punched the soldier with an invisible fist so hard that he almost folded over. Before the militant could raise an arm again, the guard stood up and pressed a button. The man tried to throw him away once again by using his telekinetic power, but this time it didn't do much. The soldier's exoskeleton suit could now absorb the power.

"Well, that's how it is then, huh?" The militant smiled and smashed the gun across the soldier's helmet. Then they went at it with a flurry of punches, kicks and jabs. Jack was incredulous. No normal humans were strong enough to stand up to even a common Sanctum soldier, but the man did, and appeared to hit the soldier blow for blow.

"It isn't possible," he heard Milly whisper.

"You bet it is."

"What should I do?"

"Run," he said, and let go of the cable.

He fell, seeing the frantic yet adorable face one last time. The ocean green eyes and the tousled red curls, dangling beside her small heart-shaped face. Before he hit the floor, a Sanctum guard grabbed her by the waist and took her away.

The pain was far from sweet, unlike the farewell. It was jarring. He almost went through a concussion when his head hit the ground. He opened his eyes, but for a few good seconds the surroundings swam. He clutched his head, and for a few moments he lay like that. When his head felt safe enough, he tried sitting up. The man across the corridor had beaten the guard down. He grinned, and started walking towards Jack.

The wall blew again. In fact, the walls blew from all directions. The fight was here now. All around him were gunshots and the electric buzz. A soldier charged down the corridor, yanked Jack by his collar, and took off running. They ran through one of the broken walls and into a room, where they came face-to-face with a girl from the other side. She was dressed in blue vest and green suit, similar to the other man.

She raised her gun, but the soldier hit it with his baton so hard that it fell, half melting and degrading. A guard or the soldier's baton of disintegration, could quite literally degrade through anything. And then he smacked it across the girl's face, which melted completely in a stream of blood and tissue right where he hit.

"KIARA!" There was a scream and the entire section of the apartment wall and everything within blew up. A man came charging. Long coat, hair messed up. No hat this time. Jack knew it. It was Brock's killer.

The soldier ran, while still dragging Jack. He left through the back exit of the apartment; but before he could drag him out, an invisible fist hit him and sent him reeling. Jack looked across: the man was coming at them. But before he could cross any distance, there were four soldiers upon him. Jack ran towards his soldier, who prised open his dented helmet. Jack gasped at two things simultaneously. First, a soldier was never supposed to take off their helmet, and second that it was…

"Alex?"

"Yes!" he said, flustered by the hit but still smiling. "Surprised to see you alive."

"And why…? How are you here?"

"Figured it was related to you when there was an emergency alarm in our base to rush to this area, so I sneaked into the armoury and stole a soldier's suit."

He then got up quickly, but the ground thrummed once again, just like it did before. The thrumming got louder and this time it was like that of an aircraft's engine.

"Knights!" Jack said, his eyes wide.

"No." Alex shook his head. "Not their ship. This is the *NightScythe*."

"So they're leaving?"

"Hopefully."

The man who was encroached by other soldiers walked towards them once again. At a closer look, the man appeared to be twenty, no older than Jack.

"Hi, my name is Maverick, and the man with me is Fred. You will have to come with us."

"I don't think so," said Jack.

"But you have to."

"You killed someone I knew, for Lord's sake."

"Who? The bartender? Well, I apologise. He was supposed to be one of us, and unfortunately the one spying on you."

The fighting stopped instantly, with Alexander's gun still having enough momentum to accidentally bump Fred, who had just joined them.

"Ughhhhhh," Fred grunted, raising his fist; but he froze when Maverick raised his hand.

"Why do you always have to stop me?" he complained.

"Well, for one, a fist for a fist engulfs the entire world in pain…"

"Enough!" cried Alexander. "What are you here for?"

"Well, we're here to rescue Jack."

"From what?"

"It is a story too long to tell. But I know he's supposed to be like us. He has the power." He looked Jack right in the eyes. "Look, this mystery that you're trying to solve…" — and then he pointed in the direction of the exit leading to the balcony, where the *NightScythe* hovered — "can be only answered there."

Jack looked at Alex, and then back at the strange faces. The face of his best friend, or the chance of escaping this world, and possibly dying the stupidest death ever? He couldn't escape without Alex, though, so he raked his mind for a possible idea, and he just got one.

"I am coming," said Jack, and he grabbed Alex's arm, following the men as they rushed towards the ship.

"Are you crazy? They will kill us!" yelled Alex, as he was being dragged.

"RETREAT!" a voice boomed like thunder, as a tall man in spectacles, in similar combat uniform to the others, and with a blond ponytail streaked with white, gathered all the members in front of the exit.

He was followed by a woman, two Asian boys and a girl who Jack didn't particularly notice. They all stopped in front of the ship, which looked exactly like its name upon a closer look: sleek, with its body and the wings shaped literally like a scythe's blade, and coloured dark as the night.

"Open the hatch. Get them in," commanded the man who'd shouted for retreat earlier.

As they got up, Alex freed himself from Jack's grip and pulled him behind his back. He then pulled his lightning-discharge rifle off its holster on his back, and was about to fire towards the ship when Maverick snapped his open palm, and the rifle flew from Alex's arms and disappeared beyond the balcony.

"No funny business," Maverick warned.

The fight was officially over for them.

Jack looked at Alex and nodded. "I will find you again when I find everything out."

With that, Maverick raised both his arms, and everything visible in the complex from the exit was covered in a swirl of dust and debris.

"Wear your helmet, and disappear inside so that no one finds you were here," Maverick told Alex, and pulled Jack along with him on the ship as the hatch closed after them.

Beyond the vile

The deck of the ship was quite small, Jack noticed. A small, rectangular room with a couple of benches, a round, big glass enclosure in the corner with enough space for a person to stand at a time. Jack had no idea what it was, but it was probably for individual teleportation, which boggled his mind. The Sanctum wasn't the only one with this technology; these guys had it, too. Besides that, on the deck there were only some panels on the wall for controlling the ship's weapons, while the flight was controlled in the cockpit leading through one of the doors.

Their leader yelled a warning, and quickly punched some buttons on the panel. Jack had felt an intense sudden headache by looking at that man and Maverick, but it was short-lived compared to the nausea of the teleportation. It was as if the surroundings had liquefied into a whirlpool and then was sucked through a drain.

No one besides him threw up, except for a girl, wiping her mouth on her blue vest. She had flowing dark hair tied in a ponytail, and startling green eyes. With a sudden shock, he realised it was the girl who

Alex had hit with his disintegration baton, causing her face to melt off.

"What in the actual hell?" was all Jack could manage to say.

"Power of illusions, man. That's my thing, to trick fools. Telekinesis is far from the only powers we have."

Her eyes drifted off to one of the Asian boys, who only now was throwing up as a delayed reaction. Those boys were actually twins at a closer look, with high cheekbones and spiked hair.

"Dude, for a soldier, being so soft doesn't suit you," said Maverick, as he stood with his arms folded.

The boy looked up, grinning. "And for a man with a big mouth and tough talk, that belly suits you."

The group burst into laughter. Maverick looked at his belly, poking through his overcoat, that was otherwise perfectly fit for him.

"We gotta cut the coffee," cackled Fred.

"All right then, it's time we got going," said the leader, and the group took their combat uniforms off and got into average civilian clothes. Maverick was the only one who wore no uniform, while the leader was revealed to be dressed in a handsome, deep-green waistcoat, and trousers, white and blue pinstripe shirt, and a blue tie beneath his combat clothing. It suited his wise, middle-aged look. The twins and the girl, and the older lady, just threw on jeans and T-shirts.

"All right, so before we leave, I am Van Vuren," said the leader. "I believe you know this pair is Maverick and Fred; the twins are called Zachary and Ferrell, even though I can't tell the difference still. The girl you know is Kiara, and the older lady is Vanesse, her mother."

"Watch your tongue, old man," scorned Vanesse, but smiled kindly at Jack. She looked like an older but almost identical copy of her daughter, or rather it was the other way around.

Van Vuren then proceeded to punch some buttons on the panel, and the hatchway unlocked with a click. It gently touched the road, with the hum of the mechanism gently fading away.

They stepped out into a junkyard, with miles of rusted-up cars, trucks and RVs stretching either side. There were even private ships, manufactured by a company called Slyce. It used to produce military-grade warships for the Sanctum, the *NightScythe* being one of them. For two hundred years, however, they had been sanctioned to only produce private ships, which obviously only the rich and the affluent population could afford. Once Jack would have loved to buy one of the models, since even the cheapest one was more comfortable than a house, and a much more exciting place to live.

He turned around to see if everyone had disembarked, and then to ask an obvious question. The question in his mind was: how could a warship in a junkyard go unhidden? However, he was entirely caught off-guard with a dozen more when he turned around. They were legitimately standing outside an RV, with no sign of a scythe-like warship.

He heard amused chuckles from Kiara and the twins, who saw his plain confusion.

"Ah, I see," he whispered after a brief pause. "No wonder it felt crammed and rectangular from the inside. You removed the flight deck and replaced it with an RV. So the RV is teleported to this junkyard, and the ship is teleported to your base. No wonder you guys are believed to be a myth."

"Wow," said Zachary, surprised. "You like a private detective or something?"

Jack simply smiled and pointed at the RV's hatchway. "That opens up like a plane hatch, rather than a normal RV door. Anyone curious would realise it…"

"Well, we've got a smart one here," said Kiara. "Kidnapping you and revealing our presence after two centuries had better be worth it, dude. Welcome home."

Jack still had a million questions as they walked back to the base. Why him? How did the organisation hide, and who were they? But he knew he would have to wait to reach the base first.

It was an hour before they reached a fairly confined boulevard in a packed area of Manhattan. Jack didn't know where exactly they were, but it was as normal and packed as Manhattan could get, all right. Not that he had ever needed to know directions; the future had perfected autonomous driving.

The group was scornful whenever they passed a subway entrance leading up to an underground network with hovering cars. Owning them was a thing for the rich people, but he would have loved to drive one as well.

It was the first time out for Kiara and the twins, and they were surprised at how much greener the world was. Sanctum had completely destroyed private housing and replaced it with skyscrapers and underground tenements, so all the new space could be reforested.

Even Jack's office tower, which soared a hundred floors besides New York's Central Park, was as deep as two hundred floors underground. So, while the surface thrived with more greenery and unadulterated landscape, the underground thrived with vast, crisscrossing lanes of roads and communities.

They had reached their place. Across the road, there were tenements painted in blue, white and occasionally golden; the colours of Sanctum. They looked no taller than a few storeys, so they probably went a dozen floors underground. The one they approached was squished between two taller ones, with only multiple floors. It was painted light blue.

Jack felt his heart pounding as they were about to enter through a rust-eaten iron gate. Maybe he should have had at least asked what their intentions were, but now he could only comply. He just hoped that Alex had reached the base safely and avoided the trouble.

The door opened up near the staircase. The first floor was visible from the ground through an old-fashioned wooden balustrade. There was a round, web-infested chandelier, a piano and some withering book shelves. On an average guess, the furniture, the wooden floor and everything else was probably a century old.

"Your friend will be all right," said Van Vuren, stopping. "He handled the situation better than I'd expect anyone to. He's spent his life believing the Sanctum's lies. When the facts which people believe to be true all their lives are proven to be nothing more than an illusion, they often go insane."

There were some mutters of agreement and assent from the group.

"Given time, you will understand it all. Do not worry; as for your friend, he will barely remember anything due to the shock and our illusions."

"Shouldn't you guys be afraid that you just revealed your presence to the world as well?" asked Jack, curious.

Van Vuren shook his head. "Trust me, Sanctum knows we exist, but we lay dormant and hidden. Anyhow, it has been a century since Sanctum took anything that seriously. Their surveillance is weaker now. They've stagnated with all their power. There are things happening which you will see with time."

Kiara growled, "I am hungry; can we please go?"

"Well, then." Van Vuren looked at Jack. "Shall we?"

Jack nodded. And so, Van Vuren led them to the gate by the staircase, and touched it gently. The lock softly clicked open.

Maverick elbowed him, smirking, and then they went down the stairs. After a couple of floors underground, they were led to a stone-made, spiralling staircase. There were no railings, which was quite frightening to think about. There were no floors either, just a spiral staircase slithering into the abyss. Strange enough, they almost seemed to be glowing with a visible aura; and even stranger, the group itself emitted a faint light. Fascinating, Jack thought, quite genuinely star-struck by them.

They all trudged down mundanely, as if the stairs were nothing extraordinary at all. He felt tensed walking down, though: one slip and he'd have nothing stopping him from falling to his death.

"Don't worry, you will not fall," Van Vuren's voice reassured from somewhere down the queue. It was so soothing factually and absolute, though, that he could have walked off into the abyss without the worry.

"Ow, my foot!" squealed someone from below, and the procession came to a halt, bumping into each other. Jack bumped into Van Vuren, who was like a wall of steel. He fell sideways, flailing his arms in panic.

But, instead of falling off, it was as if his arms just went through water, and then the watery ripples put him back on his feet. He was absolutely startled. He touched the air beyond the edge of the steps again, and it was just like touching invisible ripples of water, or really, really dense air. He poked the air, and felt it pierce and wrap around his hand.

"Yeah, it's a bit magical, you can say…" he heard Van Vuren say, and then they kept climbing down.

At some point, the stairs stopped and everyone jumped. Jack screamed, knowing well enough that the empty ledge wasn't going to comfort his plight. Nonetheless, he jumped. It felt like plunging through water, again, with no rasp of wind in his ear.

"Wooooh!" Jack cried in elation, enjoying the sensation he had never felt before. Even others joined in below him.

They soon reached the bottom, where they smoothly descended to a halt. They were now in a tiny cave, with a large gate.

There was a small pool of light, leaking from the crevices. It was dim, but enough to see the pattern on the gate. The gate itself was beige, with orange-coloured debossing on its borders. In the middle of the gate, the orange debossing curved once, like a wave, and then formed a sun. The sun itself was made with stratums of obsidian, making it a three-dimensional etching. It was simply magnificent, but it was when they walked in that Jack's mind was absolutely blown away.

It was a huge cavern. Or in Jack's perception, it was beyond description. It spread out for several square miles. But more than that, there was a community. No, an entire city; rows upon rows of linked houses, squished and stacked and leaning against each other. There were suburban houses with their decorated sidings and lawns; cosy cottages with small garden patches; flat-roofed houses; and small duplexes. It was as if an English, American and Latin American neighbourhood from the past were splattered onto a canvas. All sorts of cultures, history and atmosphere dabbed into one painting, and their aura dripping from it.

The Sanctum world was nothing like that. It was sophisticated, sparse, white and blue. That was it. Perhaps greener, but deader than a rock in its essence. All sorts of colours invigorated Jack's vision. Red, green, blue, whatever style and whims the people made their communities to be. Some were chaotically stacked like toppled dominoes and some spacious with asphalt roads in front of them.

The cavern, in its enormity, was so huge that the city itself was apparently built on carved-up hills. He even saw transcepts, spires and crosses, which he understood belonged to churches.

One church in particular caught Jack's attention. He'd seen in history books, although it didn't exist any more, due to Sanctum's demolition.

Its eight spires soared above all, with such intricate construction and magnanimity that he was just left gaping. He blankly pointed towards it, not knowing what to say.

"Sagrada Familia, an ancient, iconic church from Spain. It represents that the spirit of the old world is still very much alive here," said Van Vuren with visible pride.

"Churches, huh?" Jack asked, obviously quite ignorant of the past.

"Yes. Most of the Dark was founded by Christians, as it is an American resistance, along with a bit of everyone else. Over time, with our morale so low, people found a way to co-exist."

"I see..."

"If this city boggles your mind, then the auditorium of history will completely blow you away," said Maverick.

Not knowing what that was, Jack looked confused, and so to aid him, Vanesse suggested, "Go easy on him. Give the boy a day or two. Take him to the city maybe, show him around, find some room perhaps and have a drink."

"No," said Jack, his brows furrowed with determination. "I need to know why I am here."

Van Vuren smiled. "Very well then, if you insist, you will learn soon."

A pale girl with a curious nature

Reyn wasn't anxious for the exams, which would usually concern her. It was the time of the yearly exam. She had flipped through Maths, half-read Chemistry, half-solved some Physics equations, and left the Technology books untouched. Her prowess was in the Physical and Combat exams, and it made her proud to be in a chiselled shape. Her comely face and jet-black hair really went along with it as well.

She waited on the ground outside the Dark military school, which was a mile away from the back of the city, along with all its five hundred students. Somehow, the exams were delayed, with the professors nowhere in sight. It made her hope that they were cancelled for today, replaced by just the Combat tests. She used to be a diligent student, but being eighteen years of age, and still being prohibited from seeing the outside world, dampened her nature greatly. After all, what was the point of all this, if nothing but to be trapped like a moth in a jar?

Beside her stood her little group, the most notorious of the school. There was Lappins, a short, young Latin-African kid who was born punching keys on a keyboard. His parents were prime tech engineers of the cave, so he was raised with the knowledge of their best technology. Even now, he was surrounded by her best friend Ashley and the twins, Zachary and Ferrell, who were all vying to get some last-minute facts from him. The twins might have been masters at Combat and Warfare knowledge, but the theory was not their forte.

"God dammit," muttered Maverick, looking at his watch for the umpteenth time, waiting for something to happen. An hour had passed already.

She walked towards the group. Maverick stood at a distance, frantically flipping through the notes on his phone.

"You guys need to know, it's just too late," she said, grinning.

"Oh, look, it's the traitor who always scores high after promising not to study for a test," said Maverick, mocking her tone of speaking.

She rolled her eyes. "Ugh, not this time."

"Ha, ha. You know what? You both seem dodgy to me. Your bare minimum grade, as I overheard, is a freaking A."

"Yeah, and what do you expect to strive for, a C?" This time it was Ashley chiming in.

In the reddish-yellow hue of the artificial cave lighting, her smile looked dazzling. The sunlight really brought out her copper hair and the contrast of hazel-green eyes.

Maverick seemed to bite back a retort, as he often did against her. It made Reyn smile.

"Don't worry, you've got amazing military knowledge along with those guns," said Zachary, mocking Maverick's skinny arms.

Maverick blushed and went back to studying. It was all banter in good nature, because they all knew Maverick could hurl almost anyone with his telekinesis. Well, except for her. Her own power was summoning an invisible, protective shield. Van Vuren insisted that the power was a state of mind, which, no wonder, as reclusive as she was, only reinforced her defence.

"Speaking of exams, where is Jack?" asked Maverick suddenly.

"I reckon I will get him. I am not gonna learn anything standing here anyways," said Reyn, and walked off.

She knew where he would be: in Van Vuren's house for private tuition, which was located on a hill at the eastern backwaters of the city. Jack usually had his lessons there. She had only met him a few times since his arrival in the past few days, but never on a personal basis. She was curious about what he knew of the world outside of this cave. How mighty and beautiful the earth was on the surface, and what she wouldn't give in order to leave the cave and bathe her pale skin in real sunlight. She didn't know what his plan was, but she really intended to help him solve the mysteries.

If Jack held onto his case, it meant for her a chance to escape the Dark.

The hill was approximately twenty minutes to walk from the school. It was the sleaziest and the tallest one, towering above all the smaller ones which were around it. The view was really poetic. She could gaze at the entire city at the top, which was divided into four districts by the highways which met in the centre. She could see the school, and the vast blank back side of the cave, which was mostly shrouded in darkness.

At the left side of the city, the lake shimmered in green and slightly reddish shades under the artificial lighting. Judging by the pale, cold morning, the water was probably chilled. During the evening, from this hill you could see half the city getting darker before the rest, which she always found fascinating. It also happened to be a chaotic view of the city, due to how packed the city was, but for her that had its own beauty rather than whatever artificial world the Sanctum had built on the surface. Either way, she walked towards the house, and found the door slightly ajar.

Of course, Van Vuren's was the last house likely to be ever broken into. The murmur of two male voices engaged in a conversation became audibly clear. She could make out the deep, encompassing voice of Van Vuren, ancient and engulfing as the cave itself, against the boyish voice of Jack. The tested and learnt versus the untested and youthful.

When she reached the door, she saw Van Vuren standing in front of the holographic TV, his arms folded. Jack slouched on one of the couches in the centre of the living room. He tapped his fingers on the desk in a seamless tune.

"So, like you said, you found Maverick like me, but a year ago… working as a librarian?"

"Yes."

"And that's because we had these traces of power which link strongly with the Dark? To the aura of this cave."

"Yes. What we don't know is how and why you suddenly appeared on our radars. But why is this happening now? Well, there is more to it, but only us professors and a few elders know of it. We can't disclose it to you before we uncover what Sanctum is up to."

"Ah, so I guess that's the bit you can't tell me?"

Van Vuren nodded.

"Well, fair enough. I am satisfied with knowing that. So, what is this power? Can I possess it, too? Is this why you've been alive so long?"

"Indeed, the ones who possess power can live several life-spans of a normal person. To keep it simple, during World War Three, a group of people managed to find… an astral source of energy. A source from where our minds — or the soul, if you will — could absorb these powers. This source is called the rift. Somehow, both Sanctum and the resistances, or the first version of Dark, found them, too. Unfortunately, since the war ended, only the heir to the royal families of the Sanctum, and the heir to the Dark and other resistances can inherit it." He briefly paused, raising his hand and making those almost-invisible ripples flow around them.

"As for how to use it: it is deeply ingratiated in your state of mind and subconscious. For instance, Maverick wants to wage a war on Sanctum, and he lives to die that way. Since that's how his state of mind is, he is able to manifest the power into telekinesis; and, in rare instances, telepathy. They're the most common power which people develop, but it is extremely difficult to be as powerful as Maverick to use it. Most people in the Dark use it to boost their physical strength and bionic weapons which absorb your power." He finally finished, and smiled kindly in Reyn's direction and gestured her to sit.

She somehow always loved the welcoming feeling of being back in the class. Only a few were fortunate enough to be personally tutored by Van Vuren.

"Well, I wouldn't have expected a fat librarian to be so lethal," Jack grinned, referencing to Maverick.

Van Vuren laughed, shaking his head. "Be that as it may, we're all somewhat distinctly and predominantly inclined to accept certain ideals which remain unchanging, regardless of our age and social status. What about you, though, Jack? What do you stand for? What is your state of mind?"

"I… I don't know," said Jack. "On one hand, we have a peaceful world, where the humans aren't plagued with wars. There's no violence or fighting, there's no divisions, so in that regard Sanctum did save us. Wouldn't another war just undo everything?"

"Exactly," said Van Vuren. "But we are a population of three billion; the rest, you can guess, perished in the world war and Sanctum's malicious attempts at reducing the population ever since. I have lived a little above two centuries, and seen this world being rebuilt. There are horrors worse than imaginable that went into this. Centuries of miswritten history, of augmented literature, of deception and control which has now enthralled the newer generations. Take this, for instance: Sanctum puts all the children into boarding school until they're eighteen. Is that not cruel?"

Reyn had sort of grown wary of these conversations. "Yet you won't let me out. You talk about freedom, yet where's my freedom? This cave is hardly an ideal place."

Jack raised his eyebrows. "You don't like it here? It's pretty cool. It is actually pretty boring outside."

"Huh? You're right, but I am tired of living here. Yeah, sure, it seems gorgeous, but I don't want to be trapped here forever. I want to see the world. I want to swim in the oceans, climb over mountains… just be free."

Jack smiled. "Wow, I understand that. Well, then, the world really is beautiful outside. Perhaps one day I could take you with me?"

"Really?" Reyn beamed earnestly.

Van Vuren smiled at her reaction, but changed the topic all the same. "Well, Reyn, no theoretical exams for today. It will be done like it was in our war days: pure combat and strategy training. Go get there."

Despite herself, Reyn let loose a little shriek of excitement. The only year she'd decided to lose her motivation for the studying happened to be the best one. She tugged at Jack's coat and dragged him to join the group for this test.

Along the way, they saw Mr Smith, their physical combat training professor, absolutely yelling away on his roof. He was apparently startled awake from his sleep, and exposed in a robe, so ajar and tight that they could see it trying to escape.

"What does the funny bald guy teach you?" asked Jack.

Reyn laughed, shaking her head.

"I am serious," he said, looking innocent.

"Yeah... it's just the way you worded it. He's our teacher for physical combat training."

Jack was flabbergasted. "What? I thought it'd be Van Vuren... not him."

"Ah, you're right, kind of. Van Vuren does teach us about using power and stuff. Mr Smith is mostly about pure physical training."

"It's still weird picturing him doing flying kicks and stuff with those pudgy legs. I mean, imagine him ripping a massive hole in his shorts during a session."

Reyne laughed. "You know, for quite the thinker, you're a funny guy."

They talked further about his mystery cases, and clues, but she avoided pushing him. The last thing she wanted was to mess up how well their conversation went.

Ashley saw them from afar and beamed, waving her arm. Maverick looked up from his miserable last-minute rampage of the books and tried smiling, but as the klutz he was, he dropped the book, sending the papers fluttering everywhere. Lappy and the twins immediately sprang to help him, but just made matters worse.

"Well, they're coming. It's gonna be a special exam," Reyn told Ashley.

"Is it really?"

"Yeah, it is going to be purely combat and strategy, so like a game."

Finally, a black Cadillac pulled up in front of the school, and the seven professors stepped out of it. Van randomly climbed a boulder and made it his podium. Without further dawdling, he spoke. The voice reached each and every one of them.

"All right then, we apologise for the lateness. However, the waste of time wasn't completely in vain, for we've decided to cancel your theoretical exams — and yes, including science..."

The students erupted into a raucous applause. After a few seconds, Van raised his hand, but the crowd couldn't be silenced. He smoothly let his hand down, slid his pistol off its holster, and fired a shot in the air. The cheers turned into shrieks, before finally becoming silence. Reyn smiled. Classic Van Vuren when it came down to business.

Jack bumped into her, and she was glad to help him. Maverick cleansed his ear. The only person completely unfazed, beside Maverick, was Lex Helbert, the leader of the gang of ruffian kids called the Iron Mold. Not so unlike her own group, except her group didn't have a fancy name or a mascot. That group, especially Lex, only had the power of physicality to boost their strength, which was considered to be the poorest form of it; but he had worked himself to be strong enough to shatter ground with his bare fists.

"Well, then. Now that we've shown our gratitude for the occasion, the test is to solve a mystery. Stay in your groups and teams, and remember, you can fully sabotage your opponents to reach the end goal. It is a test of morals, diligence and intelligence; all the same, much more practical, like our past. When our education was strictly military. The scythe will cut the enemy, while the sickle will strike from the shadows."

Van Vuren then stepped off his makeshift rock podium, leaving a holographic projector there, before he left in the Cadillac, along with the professors. It looked like that would be enough to deliver the task.

The holograph flickered to life with a video. It showed a man with yellowish skin and yellowish sickly eyes. The eyes were unnaturally wide and narrow, like slits. The nose was long and narrow. And the lips, yet again, were thin and very wide. It was like a caricature. The man seemed to be speaking something, but there was no audio. Overall, it was uncanny and unsettling. And then the recording stopped, fading into a black backdrop, with a voice speaking, "Find what this is. You may now begin to discuss. The rules will be delivered shortly."

"Yeah, this is definitely strange..." Jack mumbled.

"Yeah, this really was strange," she replied.

"No. Not this." Jack reached close to her ear and whispered, "It's almost like they're expecting a war and preparing us for it. I mean, the parade could be targeted to kill the Paragon, the royal families, the whole army at the same time."

Reyn's eyebrows shot up in surprise. That was a gutsy assumption. But before she could give it any more thought, the whistle blew, and the groups started scrambling. No one knew what the clip meant, creating arguments and chaos.

"It's too loud!" squealed Ashley.

"Let's move away a bit," said Maverick, and they followed. They had to put some distance from the mass in order to gather their thoughts.

"Well, then, let us ask the same. Whence does the clip come from, and where shall our curiosity lead?"

"Stop it, Maverick. No time for your semantics," Ashley groaned.

"Why'd they show us footage of a random conversation?" Jack asked them.

Reyn had a sudden thought. "It's a mystery case, and what are most mysteries typically about? Murder."

Jack smiled at her. "Brilliant. That may or may not be the case, but since it was from a third-person perspective, and the footage seemed bloody distorted… I think it might be a recording. We were asked to find what this is, not who it is."

There were cheers of agreement in the group, but Maverick remained sceptical. "Wait, wait, wait. Even if we're right, where can we find the recording in this whole damn city?"

"If you ignored his face, and saw the surroundings, you could see spires behind his hat. So it was shot right in the area behind the replica church," said Jack.

But that was the farthest area of the city from their current position. If what they discovered was nothing but a far-fetched guess, they'd lose time running there.

Reyn had an idea. "It's simple! We need somewhat of a high ground, so we just parkour over the rooftops and get there fast."

Before they could plan any further, the holograph promptly came to life with audio once again. "If you're done teaming up, then there's one last rule to be delivered. The four highways are the only neutral areas. The four districts, however, can be captured by any team, which they can subsequently own and defend. The team to finish the objective first shall gather at the four horsemen roundabout."

The crowd had momentarily been smothered by pin-drop silence. Suddenly, Reyn was aware of the eyes of all her team-mates on her.

"Well, then, let's just run. If Jack is right about the scene behind the church, then we should conquer the American District." She sprinted, not glancing back at any of them, knowing well enough that they were following. In fact, she didn't even need reassurance, as she practically heard hundreds of feet stomping the ground with a penchant for glory.

Vendors of all kind

Lappy felt his feet stomping against the cobblestones. They had entered well into the American District, passing streets of asphalt with posh, classy houses and sleek, white villas. They passed a few schools on the way. His lungs were burning already, and his shins were aching. The bile already tinged his mouth. He surely had to glance sideways, at the cost of losing his dwindling concentration, in an effort to see if it was time to halt and recuperate yet. It was futile; their expressions showed anything but effort.

To his left were Reyn, the twins and Ashley, all busy making their way through the haphazard, obnoxious markets which cluttered the streets. Every now and then he'd hear them grunt, when hit by a corner of a fruit cart, or crudely thatched wooden awnings, which were notorious for hindering the public path.

He was glad that he didn't have to be the one to clear the room; he just followed, barely keeping up. Much of the room was cleared by Maverick, who was… just jumping like a frog, since he couldn't run, or fly. Least bit he could do was appear like a not-so-incredible hulk.

To his right was Jack, who was absolutely enthralled by the wild, obfuscation that Dark was as a place. Lappy could understand that the outside world was all blue and white and pristine, while this rookery was an utter, nauseating disgrace. Lappy almost threw up, when, through their marathon of the food street, fragranced with stew shops and freshly baked goods from the bakeries, they suddenly ended up passing by a home next to a pooled-up pothole. It had a stench which could permanently murder someone's olfactory senses.

A stout, middle-aged lady with a large, grey bun and a chin wider than a mountain, was berating the rather zoned-off sweeper.

"Hey, you, I warned ya yesterday to clean this big pile of filth…"

"Yes, I know, ma'am…"

"Then why is it all pooled-up here? Get back to work before I dip my broom in this goo and smack it on ya face!"

Lappy laughed, hearing the verbal onslaught slowly faint away in the hubbub. Jack heard it, too, grinning from ear to ear. They made it out of the chaotic market place and made it into another, more demure residential and schooling area. They passed by a few Catholic schools, which didn't seem to faze Jack whatsoever, despite having never seen them through his life.

The housing here was different to the posh area which they had passed through. Some homes were tall, lanky and slanted, some completely awkwardly designed. But unlike the posh area with modestly constructed villas, these were bright and colourful.

"This place is so lawless," whispered Jack, but in a tone which meant that he invited that freedom.

Lappy wanted to speak, but he'd end up sounding like a car breaking down from exhaustion.

"What's up? Already tiring out?" he heard Reyn taunt, but it was meant for Jack.

"Oh no, not at all. I can keep up and I don't even have your powers," Jack called back.

The twins counted down to tree, and the members with power sprinted beyond a human pace. Their hands, instead of being balled up, became pronated, with their palm facing their back, as if to use the ripples to thrust them. Their strides became long and quick like a cheetah, as they were thrust forward with superhuman speed. Jack seemed surprised, realising that they were saving their power so far. Hem too, attempted a full-throttled sprinting, but clearly couldn't keep up beyond a dozen metres.

Lappy just let it go, and slowed down to a walk instead. At the end of the street, however, at an intersection, they all seemed to rendezvous and discuss something. They then broke up, and all the power users left Jack and ran to the left side.

Lappy was glad: now he would feel less incompetent. Jack almost forgot Lappy and began jogging away, but Lappy attempted his best shout, "Ughhh, stobbbppp!" Clearly it wasn't much of a shout, or even a traditional shout known to man. Either way, it made Jack turn around in surprise.

"You okay?"

Lappy made an even more incomprehensible noise. He couldn't speak, but he understood the startled expression on Jack's face. His panting really did sound like an old man going through a stroke. He cinched down, clutching his knees. Stopping after such a gruelling marathon made his mind blissfully march forward, while his body struggled to remain stationary.

"I… I will get you water." Jack jogged up to a water cooler some distance away, outside a small public garden, and grabbed a plastic cup from the stack to fill it.

After Lappy was done sipping it away and recovering his breath, he really had to ask, "So where did the guys go?"

"They're approaching the area we saw in the recording."

"The paradise street?"

"Yeah, must be it. I am not good at remembering directions anyhow."

Lappy raised an eyebrow. "But Van Vuren said you have an excellent memory, comparable only to me."

Jack scratched his head. "Well, there are just certain things I feel like my mind gets stuck upon and then things become foggy. If I try to force it, it stops making sense."

"Oh... I understand, I guess. So where are we going?"

"We are both left to patrol the entire district."

Lappy looked down at himself, and then at Jack, to make a point. "Are you sure? I don't think we two will be any good if any gang comes over to ravage our area."

"No, we will not be, which is why I have a better idea."

"What is it?"

"Haven't had a pint in a while. You wanna?"

And then they were walking down the street to an inn, at noon. But what was to stop them? The place was timeless of itself. Lappy felt great; it was like walking beside an older brother, or an adventurous cousin ready to do something crazy. Lappy was only sixteen, looking up to others. He glanced at Jack again; tall, lean, with long hair which waved majestically with every step, a multiple prize-winner for his investigative works; and, unlike Lappy, he was athletic, despite not having interest in sports.

"I hope I can be this cool in a few years," he muttered under his breath.

Jack gasped a little when he heard it. "Huh? But you're the most intelligent kid that there is."

"Yeah, I may be. But there are all these cool people at school, and then the smart ones. Somehow, the smart ones are usually also very cool and popular. No one talks to me that way, until they want some help to get their work done. I am basically an ampersand between the words."

Jack laughed. "That was an interesting analogy. Like an ampersand, huh? — everyone uses you, but very few acknowledge it."

Lappy grinned. "I am surprised you got the joke. Usually I have to dumb down my humour."

Jack mussed Lappy's dreadlocked hair. "Worry not, youngling, I've had my own moments of anagnorisis often."

Lappy made a face. "Wait, what?"

"See, now this moment was your peripeteia," said Jack, grinning. But before Lappy could whine any further, Jack marched forward, presumably towards the outdoor bar across the street with the barrels of fresh cider being rolled in from a truck.

Jack took a sharp sip and sighed with satisfaction. And then he chugged the whole pint down and ordered another. Lappy could only mournfully stare at his own pint, which was too strong just for a deep gulp even.

"Been a while since I got to chug down one of these." Jack burped as he waited.

Lappy laughed, taking a gulp himself, only to burp even louder from the retaliation by his body.

Jack raised his eyebrows, and then they both laughed.

When they were done, the bartender deducted the bill from a note of one Revol, the currency of the Dark, and placed a few copper uprises and silver idils back. Five uprises made one Revol, and each uprise was twenty idils.

"Man, everything here is so cheap. I exchanged my money for Revols today. Each dollar happened to be worth ten Revols."

Lappy almost choked mid-gulp. "Are you for real? This means that here you're a millionaire?"

"I sure am. I already bought a house with a new computer, connections and everything. I do find it weird, though, that you have these hefty physical things for money! It's so funny and fascinating. Up there we only have digital currencies, and that's it."

Lappy bitterly placed his empty pint down. "Well, do invite me to play games with you then sometimes."

"No problem. My house is on the hill next to Van Vuren's..." said Jack, pointing roughly towards south-east, the backwaters of the city where it crept up the hills. The houses were fairly expensive there, for the location and placement.

An hour passed by, with them just boringly patrolling the streets. So far, they had encountered only two skirmishes. Once, when Iron Mold had run into the rookery, but were met by the 'hype-men' crew, led by the kids of British descent. Needless to say, it was a glorious showdown of the Yanks-vs-Brits tradition. However, they took each other out, and Lappy and Jack could do nothing but watch the carts flying, the pans and pots hurling, and broken wooden structures falling from the sky. But that was about it; they could only wish they knew what their team was doing.

"Jack, what if some group has already solved the mystery while our team is roaming somewhere, completely clueless?"

Jack shrugged. "Not possible. We should've seen a red flare if someone had solved it already, or a green flare if our team needed help. I am sure Reyn and Maverick will figure it out."

Speaking of which, however, there was a sudden red flare... followed nigh immediately by a green flare. Jack glanced at Lappy, and he glanced back, just as alarmed. They both wordlessly sprinted in the direction, marvelling at the coincidence.

They ran through every street possible, some laden like a typical outdoor market, and some infested with kids playing soccer. Jack, in particular, ran twice into awkwardly swinging clothesline extending from the homes. The second time he ran into one of the lines, it was a blue baby overall, and for whatever reason it was wet. It made Jack's silky hair stick to his face. There was never a fury that Lappy had ever witnessed than seeing something ruin Jack's hair.

They were almost outside of the rookery, and moving towards the paradise street, when out of a small adjoining alley stepped Lex Helbert.

He was six foot five, with a chest the size of a barrel, and arms the size of pythons. He wore a denim bib with a white T-shirt within, clad so tightly around his skin that his triceps looked like jutting hills. "Where is the recording?" he grunted.

"What recording?" Jack asked, as if he were clueless.

"Your team found one. It is a part of this stupid puzzle."

There were no further explanations. Lappy glanced at both of them. Jack clearly gauged the situation.

"To be fair, we don't even know what you're talking about," said Jack, assuming an unconcerned stance and dusting his coat off. He stood completely relaxed.

Lex bared his teeth and slammed his fist in his palm. "Are you sure? There's none of your mates, that guy Maverick or Reyn to protect you."

"Yes, I am. They all left us both here to defend ourselves. We don't have any powers, as you see."

Lappy actually saw a second of remorse on Lex's face. "Ah, those assholes. I don't have any of that fancy power, either. But you can try and beat yourself up every day, like I did."

"Power of physicality," muttered Lappy.

Lex looked at him. "What's that? Yeah, that is it. It sure does sound weak, and less fancy, but it gets work done. Better than being the weaklings that you both are now."

Lappy felt as if he was being stabbed. He wasn't even sure if he could achieve a power of physicality in strength, as even that was a hit and miss chance for those who had failed in every other discipline. In their group, both Zachary and Ferrell were not able to channel their power into telekinesis like Maverick, so training to synergise with any deadly weapon which could shoot energy was a technique that most power users ended up with. But inheritance of power was subject to chance, and his parents were already very weak users.

Jack clearly ignored the remark, and tapped his temple. "I don't need that futile power. Look where it is getting everyone. Now make way for us, for we both have the power of common sense to solve this damn mystery!" And then he grabbed Lappy's arm, and bolted.

The shock was jarring, as it almost pulled Lappy's shoulder from its socket. They heard Lex scream and rip out and throw a wooden beam. They both ducked, but the onslaught continued. Lex picked up crates and barrels, and entire stalls stocked with vegetables, and hurled them. The street was in chaos. People were bolting off in all directions. Many even cheered; the ones that spectated from their roofs and balconies. These soldiers were their heroes, after all.

Eventually, Jack's grip broke, as a motorcyclist suddenly split them apart. Jack jumped over the barricades on a road and kept going, while Lappy had no choice but to run around it. He peered back in a frenzy: Lex was still charging, and getting alarmingly closer to him. Jack was already getting too far ahead. It seemed inevitable that he was going to be caught alone and would have to work with the Iron Mold kids.

He glanced back again; Lex was barely ten metres behind. Lappy panicked, and smashed his knee against a barrier on the road. He stifled a cry as tears flooded his eyes. He tried to stumble forward, but an oncoming car's rear-view mirror hit him in the ribs. He had no sense of direction now, and stepped into a pothole. He fell face first, with his teeth hitting the road. The deluge of pain broke through, and he almost fainted. Any moment now, he'd be grabbed by the terrifying, asphyxiating grip of Lex's hands.

But nothing really followed. As the tears rolled away from his eyes, and his vision cleared, all around him was just chaos. He was still lying in the same spot. He looked to his left: the street was completely empty of people, but it was swarmed by kids. Lex was fighting members of the hype-men crew. Someone had stolen a military jeep from the armoury warehouse at the far east of the city, and another group was firing energy-blasting guns. Zachary and Ferrell were combating kids from other groups, all equipped with crowbars and baseball bats.

Their synergy was majestic, as always. Zachary ducked, jumped back, and went into several backflips to dodge an onslaught of rocks, while Ferrell quickly jumped on a car and caught the swinger with a bat right on his surprised face. Then Zachary grabbed a baton and threw it, which whizzed past Ferrell and hit someone else who was trying to swing at Ferrell's knees from the back.

Lappy stood up, flinching. His knee didn't feel right, making his leg wobble. He carefully tried not to place his weight on that foot, and dusted off his black tracksuit. Before he could further inspect his surroundings, the havoc just went up a notch. A wall from the backyard of a house blew apart and Reyn was hurled backwards, caving into a car. Her black, leather jacket was gone, exposing a deep blue tank top. Her arms were all cut up and bruised. She stayed like that for a couple of seconds, the hair falling over her face. She then grunted and stood up, marching forward.

"Oh boy, bad news!" muttered Lappy, and sure enough, there were all kinds of screams as she walked back into the broken-into house, followed by a torrent of groups, boys and girls alike, flooding the street. He was terrified but glad, grinning to himself. He then turned around, looking in the direction where Jack was supposed to be. Even he was fighting, ducking, dodging, and throwing combinations of right crosses and left hooks.

Lappy suddenly realised that Kiara had joined as well. She was Vanesse's daughter, and, as such, usually stuck with their group. She had already graduated, so she was not a part of the competition. But she was always eager to have some fun.

She charged at Jack to test him, attempting a roundhouse kick. He leaned back instinctively, and as soon as she was done with the spin, Jack pulled her head and went in for an uppercut. She stumbled back, with her lip busted. She flipped aside a lock of hair, and then grinned, beckoning him with her hand.

Lappy ran towards them and cried, "Stop it, you two!"

Kiara made a face. "Why?"

Jack was panting, but managed to grin. "You want to go again?"

"Nah, he ruined it," she said, curling her lip.

"Well, then, what's happening?" Lappy addressed the elephant in the room.

"Basically, our group found this recording behind the church, which automatically sent this red flare up to the sky. Things went crazy then, so I ran up here as soon as I saw a green flare from my window," Kiara explained to them.

They were all wondering what they were supposed to do next, until suddenly, Lappy saw Maverick on one of the taller apartment buildings, followed by a small helicopter. He gestured the camera man to lean forward a little more to capture the street footage.

"Well, then, the Maverick is here! It's a pun," Lappy said. The entire street groaned in response.

"Well, now. Simmer down, simmer down, young people. We're on the news!"

"Seriously?" Kiara swore, exasperated. "Are you serious, Maverick?"

Maverick paid no heed to her, but kept talking gibberish for a distraction. He inconspicuously placed his hands on his temple, and Lappy felt Jack tugging at his sleeve. Seemed like he had received a telepathic message. He then told Lappy and Kiara what they were supposed to do.

"Okay, Lappy, you know what do. Our devices have been cut off from the internet service and networks. Hacking our way into any network is available, and send our team a group message..."

"I can't... that's cheating."

He got a small clout on his head from Kiara. "Just do it, you nerd. Of all the lame things, you pull an ethical excuse."

Lappy blushed, then pulled out his device, and immediately his mind felt as if it was being washed over with dopamine; doing the thing he loved the most. But he didn't have to hack in; he just enabled his private network to reach the group. All the members across the street glanced at each other as they felt their phones notifying them.

Jack then leaned in and whispered in Lappy's ear, "Tell them to secretly back out. We group together and run from the rooftops, towards the four horsemen roundabout."

They peered across the street for confirmation, then. Ashley looked at Reyn, and they backed off, holding hands. Zachary and Ferrell slowly dropped their bats and tapped the stolen military jeep near them. They would clear out anyone who'd try to stop the group from retreating, and then would join the group.

They heard the slight ruffling of feet behind them then. Reyn and Ashley were both here. It was time to get away. They all slowly receded, hoping well that Maverick had distracted the street just long enough with his false rambling.

"Well, then. This was the real task! All of that had to do with this one verse from the Bible… So, to solve this convoluted mess… uh, we have to go to the second floor of the church and find the metaphor."

"What a load of bollocks!" someone cried across the street.

"Well, if I was lying, why would the official news helicopter support me?"

"I don't know what this man has been trying to say for the past five minutes, but we were just following him for news coverage…" yelled the helicopter man.

There was a momentary silence, until someone on the street asked where the two girls and the twins went.

Maverick swore and jumped away from the ledge, disappearing from sight.

"Go!" screamed Reyn, and they sprinted for an apartment building, running up the flight of stairs. Lappy heard the hordes of feet thunder behind him, and everyone jumped on the pursuit. He glanced back one last time, before disappearing up the staircase.

They were at the roofs now; sprinting, climbing, and launching across the tops. The twins had joined them shortly after; they had driven the car through the street, scattered everyone who tried to chase the group, and parked it as a blockade to stop the mass from climbing the stairs. Lappy was neither strong nor agile enough to navigate the terrain himself via parkour, so he was hauled onto Reyn's back, as she effortlessly climbed and gracefully tackled all the obstacles. She hopped across parapets surefooted, maintained her balance on roof tiles, and caught balustrades with iron grip on jumps. Once or twice he heard her grunt as the jump would end in a crash against the ledges.

He still marvelled at what privileged kids with power could do. Jack, too, seemed to be doing well, for someone who had no power. Soon, as they reached closer to where the North highway met the cross-section in the middle of the city, he could see the four horsemen roundabout.

Inside, was a memorial garden with a moat and four curved bridges, leading to the most exotic and vibrant garden known to man; with flamboyant flowers of such diversity, each obtained from different continents, with many that would naturally flourish in the most contrasting climates. It was a very opulent commemoration, portraying the four founders of the Dark city, who found this cave two hundred years ago. It was Lappy's favourite part of their history, to imagine what it would have been like to lose their fourth and final war, and desperately retreating to another world as humanity's only remaining hope.

In this circular garden within the moat stood four black, massive statues of the founding horsemen of the cave, and Lappy knew everything about them.

In fact, one of them was Van Vuren, the commander and strategist. The leader was Ernaline Tora, a wild, soulful girl who was a savage power user, a healer, and a doctor with multiple doctorates, and an expert in infectious diseases and microbiology. She actively counteracted during her life to stop Sanctum's biological genocide.

Then there was Alward Savage, and, just like his name, he was a raider, tasked to forage food recourses and destroy the means of sustenance for the enemy. And Grim, someone vastly introverted and vastly feared for his thirst for war. No one despised the Sanctum more than him, which is why he was the voice of the people — but, as the saying goes, anger and vengeance, given time, destroys the vengeful more than the perpetrator. This is why Van Vuren was there, to give reason to Grim's voice, and to stop people from placing their hope in someone's passion for destruction.

And finally, right in the centre of the roundabout and the four statues, was a faceless figure carved from a tree and shaped with vines. He was the original founder, who was known for his love of topiary and nature. He was the one who gathered armies all over the world during World War Three and found Dark to fight the Sanctum.

Suddenly, Reyn stopped and turned out, and asked Lappy to get off her. Lappy shook his head, feeling stupid for spacing out — but that came natural for being a deadweight during a mission.

He hopped from her back, feeling as fresh as ever — maybe less nauseous for finally not seeing death three storeys down with each of her jumps. It seemed that Jack was the one who had originally stopped, with a leg planted on the ledge. He seemed to be thinking of something.

"What happened?" she asked him.

"Why are we going towards the roundabout?"

"Because it is the main neutral zone and maybe the test ends by reaching there?" Reyn suggested.

"No, no! Why do you think the test leads us back to there?"

"I... don't know," she admitted.

"Think back to Van's speech. He said this was a test of morals, group work and intelligence… to be like Grim's sickle and scythe. Something to do with history."

"So something related to the Dark?" Reyn groaned, stretching from all the exhaustion.

Jack nodded. "Yeah, I thought about it. Van Vuren told us about the test being a throwback to history, and a test of morals. So far, we've achieved the group work, now for the history…"

Lappy quickly remembered their historical chant. "In 2030, the year when several rebel armies ranging from American anarchists, European, and the Latin resistances, found their backs to each other on an increasingly scarce land, as Sanctum plundered through the peaceful countries and scorched them…"

"But soon, they came together under one command, as their morals bound them all together, and so, the biggest resistance named the Dark was found." The statement was finished by him, the twins, Ashley, Kiara and Reyn together. It was like their oath, their pride and joy. This was their roots and where they came from. This was their country, and their chant for patriotism. From somewhere, Maverick, too, came, his arms raised by his side, and his palms splayed to propel him upwards.

"So," said Reyn, "you think we have to chant this together as a group at the roundabout as the final part of the test?"

"Yeah, I think so," said Jack.

Maverick's presence meant that he didn't come alone. As, across the highway, they saw Lex, who jumped on a ledge, and then jumped straight at them. Reyn raised her arm and splayed her palms. Lex hit an invisible shield mid-air, his face flattened like hitting a glass window. Maverick swiped his arms through the air, and sent him flying across the road, where he thudded against a roof, and fell into an alley beyond their view.

"So, the plan is to reach the roundabout, yes?" asked Kiara.

Maverick nodded. "That's what I told Jack by telepathy back there; but I don't know what to do after we reach there."

"Don't worry," said Jack. "We discussed it. I think we have to chant the history as the final step, all together."

But they didn't have time, as the highway in front of them now was flooding with a crowd of five hundred. The group quickly slid off the ledge as Reyn cushioned their fall through her power, and then they ran towards the roundabout.

Lex joined the crowd behind, crying bloody murder. Kiara turned back and raised her arms and the crowd turned into a stampede as her illusion threw everyone off. Somehow, Lex charged through while still blinded, grabbed one of her fists and crushed it. Kiara cried in pain. When Lex found his vision cleared, his face suddenly changed, seeing what he just did. Ashley ran back to Kiara, placing a hand on her fist to heal her. She then slowly supported her back to the roundabout, where the group had already gathered.

They repeated the chant together, and then kneeled. Ever so slowly, with the sound of a large boulder moving, the statue of Grim turned to face them. Maverick stood up and walked towards the statue, and then finally placed the recording at the circular base.

From the east main road, the professors emerged. Van Vuren led them, followed by Vanesse, and then Mr Smith. Four more professors followed: Miss Halle of History, Mr Hames of Technology, Miss Ernaline for Languages, and Miss Tora for Maths. These last two were sisters, the descendants of Ernaline Tora herself. The spectators were jam-packed on the roofs and the streets to witness the moment of celebration.

They all kept watching intently… and after a seemingly perpetual wait, something happened. Lappy couldn't see what, but Maverick stepped back, visibly mystified. And then he saw it. The statue's arm moved, as if somehow the stone had been brought to life. It lowered both its arms, one holding a scythe and the other holding the sickle.

Maverick reached up, and the statue let go of the scythe. Maverick then received the sickle from its other hand.

Maverick glanced around nervously at first, everyone remained silent, but then he slammed the scythe into the ground and raised it into the air.

The crowd burst into applause. The kids, the spectators perched on their roofs and the road, and the teachers themselves cheered.

Lappy was hoisted up by Jack and his team-mates as they all celebrated. He felt absolutely ecstatic. No one but their group had been able to figure out even half the mystery. Jack looked up to Lappy, as he was perched on his shoulders, and raised the stone sickle with his other hand.

"How ironic is it?" he called to Lappy. "He was called a young Grim, and he's the one to get the scythe!"

There were fireworks from above, and the student crowd was met with the spectators passing jugs of water and band aids.

But the celebrations became short-lived when Lex charged towards the roundabout with wounded pride. Maverick held up his hand in anticipation, in case Lex wasn't stopped. It was Jack who ran and tried to talk sense into him.

"Lex, wait! Don't let your insecurities blind you..."

Lex grunted and backhanded Jack away. He hit the kerb with a crunch on his elbow and shrieked.

The professors did not interrupt yet. The crowd saw the fight and broke into even more enthusiastic applause.

Maverick raised a hand, but Lex slammed his foot into the ground, and the shock disrupted Maverick's focus, causing him to fall. Reyn climbed over the bridge and stood at the outer circle of the moat, and held both of her arms in front of her. Lex pounded furiously on the invisible shield in front of him. Each strike, she jittered with the shock. She bent down, her arms still up. They were shaking uncontrollably now, but then Lex finally stopped, taking a few steps backs, before charging.

BOOM!

Something just rushed next to Reyn, and Lex was shot fifty feet into the air, before he crashed on to the ground. There, standing beside her, wielding the sickle, was Jack. He looked normal, except there was a darkness, as dark as the colour of the sickle, which had crept up his arm.

Lex got to his feet, unsure of what to do. The light around Jack seemed to be bending like a whirlpool, while tendrils of shadows spread from him. There was a scintillating burst of light, like flashes from a camera, and then Lex was dropped.

And then that was it. Jack dropped the sickle, staggering, while the crowd cheered for their group again. The professors finally stepped in and organised the kids to be walked back to the school.

Lex and the Iron Mold were put into detention. The group surrounded Jack, who was fine, but did not remember what happened. The group proceeded to enjoy their victory, but Lappy knew what he'd just seen was far from something he was going to forget soon.

A knight's lament

Arch-knight Griffith Rosendale, head of the seven Holy Knights, under service for almost one hundred years, heard the title resonate in his head like a million times before. Yet it felt exceedingly withering, an empty chant, a sentence with little meaning left with each passing day.

He stood looking through the window of his Knight's chamber. The window looked over the expanding horizon, as the Citadel of the Sanctum hovered in the sky.

He remembered the memories more vividly than he had ever before. A lean, young boy, dressed under the plump velvet robe of the Rosendale family, stood in the bleached white cathedral of Paragon's citadel. He was of the rare few who'd ever witnessed the Lord Paragon's sight with his own eyes. He was youngest of the men to be ever made a knight and an Arch-knight in all four centuries, yet the title meant little to him as it did before. After all, it was only a short time before his duty would be coming to an end.

Yet, something irked him, something that he'd rather deal with now before it would be too late. If he did not do it now, he'd never have a chance to do it again. Simply because, while the rest of the six Holy Knights would have been retired to the citadel, in the final parade the Arch-knight himself would have to kneel in front of Paragon, where he would be absolved from duty and would disintegrate into blue light. It was meant to symbolise the transcending of a soul beyond human reach. He still remembered vividly when he was knighted at the last parade a century ago. He was a little over a hundred back then, very young and youthful as a power user.

It wasn't the death which scared him, though; truth be told, the life-span he had experienced already felt more than enough. He was fairly alone when it came to having this perspective, however; the royal families of the Sanctum and the power users always took pleasure in their undying selves.

For him, though, it felt much too burdening, like him being the most beautiful man on earth, and also the most physically powerful. He slumped at the edge of his bed and took off his gauntlet. From his wrist to the tips of his fingers, the palm of his hands were scarred. The lines were crisscrossing each other as if like a mass of pale centipedes.

He clenched his fist and then put on his beautiful gauntlet once again, feeling the safety of it. Then, he gritted his teeth and walked towards the gate of his chamber. It was eight in the evening, and his appointment time. The appointment that he had so direly wanted for a long while.

He had to navigate deep into the underground; a restricted area of the citadel. Given the choice, he'd rather always avoid being anywhere near the basement level. It was cold, eerie and dilapidated. No people lived there, except for the person he was going to see. Finally, after navigating through, and avoiding the places that he considered filled with those wretched creatures, he reached the tunnel leading up to the gate. It was a solid steel, blue metal gate with the Sanctum's golden eye symbol. The eye blinked, and the gate burst into a thousand shards. He flinched; like he always did at the sheer surprise of it, despite having seen it several times before. The corridor stretched in front of him. Steel blue tiled and as cold as ice, like the many labs located in this place. What the labs contained, he didn't know. He shivered without a reason, which was a testament to the eeriness of this place.

As he stepped in, the shards of the gate, like the fragments of a magnet, were pulled back into one piece, and the gate was re-formed as impeccably as ever. He sighed, navigating the last few corridors with heed. The walls were painted yellow, with white marble floor. Just plain tunnels, occasionally stacked with wooden crates.

He always had an unsettling feeling in his gut when he came to these corridors.

Finally, he found the door. Just a regular door like any other, but it was the door leading to his destination.

He breathed deeply, and then knocked, fully knowing from experience that at one time there was no answer for hours on end, after which he was told to just walk in. And so he did, turning the knob and slowly creaking the door open. It opened to nothing but a gaping maw of darkness, with the only luminous sources being a row of monitors set on a table, attached to servers and a super-computer. Facing them was a single black chair in the middle.

The chair slowly turned, with nothing but two hollow eyes to be seen.

"You finally walk in."

The knight saw a greasy long grin beneath the pair of eyes.

"Yes… My Lord. I did, like you stated previously." He had goose-bumps all over his body.

There was no further reply, just a deep, unrelenting stare, so the knight decided to continue himself. "If I may be allowed, I am here to ask why the murder of this man named Allen is being avoided. Did we forget that this man was a part of…?"

"Cease to exist."

The knight stuttered, "P-pardon me, My Lord?"

"I know what this man meant to you, and what his death means to the stability of our world… but as per your orders, you shall forget it."

The knight lost his temper. "Did you forget that I was the one who you used to crush the Dark? The least

I deserve is to know why there is being no justice served for the man who meant so much to me."

There was no reply except for another long, gaping, unending stare. The knight's fists shook with adrenaline and anger. It would have been blasphemy to think that, there and then, he could have smashed the face in front of him if he wanted. But he quickly shook off the thought. There was nothing he could do. He wanted to move the conversation, with perhaps an, "I solemnly apologise, my Lord", but he couldn't speak. He simply shut the door and walked away, each step feeling heavier, with the yellow walls feeling closer than ever before. He couldn't breathe, as if the walls had grown cold, jagged teeth, waiting to pierce him dare he slow down.

The maglev seamlessly came to a stop. It was four in the morning, when people solemnly used a station. He had escaped the citadel, only to travel to London by himself. He slid one of his jacket sleeves a little to view the time from his watch. The cool metallic touch to his skin and the reflected station lights felt satisfying to him. He always preferred his watches to be gold, because, much like it, he happened to possess exquisite beauty.

Two people had boarded the train when he reached it. To avoid them, he picked his favourite middle compartment with his favourite place of seating. He looked at the dark window, and saw his luscious hair and features tucked below a large cap. He wore a brown leather jacket, and simple denim jeans. It was casual. Very casual. At least for him: he rarely had the pleasure of wearing ordinary human clothing.

He took his cap off, and let the thick silvery locks cascade to his shoulders. They were his trademark, and although his perfect facial features were unavoidable, he could still get away with public appearances in this clothing. The salience of giving up his cape and brooch, heraldic breastplate, and grieves and the gauntlets, to dress mundanely and disappear like a ghost away from everything, felt so relieving and addictive. He craved this sensation; the sensation of being an ordinary human.

He sighed deeply, sinking into the snug recliner seat. The air was cold yet pleasant to breathe. The train was meant to reach London from the station in Paris. If all went well, he'd never have to hear from the Lord in the citadel again. He had less than a month before the parade would reach and commence in America, so he could already picture how it would be like being absolved from the duty.

He didn't know what to feel between fear and regret, but he did feel determination. He was going to at least make some people answer for the murder of his father, which was somehow covered up by the Sanctum itself. His real father was none other than Allen, the farmer from Kansas, an ex-member of the Dark. And it was entirely his mother's fault for being involved with him. She was one of the four mothers of mercy, Angaria Storm, and the mother appointed over Sancta America. Had it not been for Paragon taking him from his father and switching him with the legitimate son of Lord Rosendale in his crib, he'd most probably have been killed as an infant.

It is why he had never liked his mother. The entire royal families of the Sanctum, in fact, were indulgent, ignorant, involved in such things that… he shuddered to think of it. He wasn't into their behaviour, and felt that they went against oaths of the book of Sanctum.

During his reign, though, he had somewhat tried to make the control over the public lenient. It was not something which Sanctum knew of, but something he was able to do by reducing the potency of the aethernet; a network of satellites which monitored the public through Common Registry.

Not that the royal families would care; they had lost their grip after centuries, mostly because Paragon had been seen only twice in the last two centuries. There was no shepherd to herd the sheep, and the Lord who lived in the citadel, well, the knight would rather not even think of him.

But, despite being a bastard born, and awakened to the realities of the Sanctum, he respected the Paragon and him only, for he would have been killed in infancy without his help.

Long ago he would have revelled in being the most fearsome of the last four Arch-knights, but not any more. He was the cause of Dark's crushing defeat in their final uprising, thinking it was for the good of the people. How naïve of him back then to think that.

He convinced himself that he had no regrets, but only now did he realise that he respected the Dark. He respected anyone that chose freedom and their own way, unlike him, who had been bound in his prison of jewels for two centuries.

His head rested against the seat, and soon the snug surroundings took him to the land where the dreams rushed back, fresh as a rain.

"This is the best!" he heard a girl cackling in the distance.

It was a surprisingly cool June morning in Kansas. The lush green grass danced with the breeze. He ran towards the noise of the cackle, and jumped down a little ledge. There were many kids playing there, but she was unlike any of them. She was so strong, and so agile. Like a beautiful cat, he thought. It was where the forest began, and the farm ended, that she came into view. She swung herself up on a branch, and then jumped, somersaulting in the air, and landing gracefully right in front of him.

She wore his favourite tank top, red in the middle and black on the sides. He looked at himself: a denim bib and a grey T-shirt. Crude as his father in every sense of fashion.

Griffith tried to backflip once, but he smacked his face in the mud. It was disgusting. He wished then that he could go back to his room in the citadel. But he didn't want to appear like a weakling. A behaviour which his mum would severely belittle.

The girl flicked her hair, grinning widely, with dimples appearing on her cheeks. Sometimes, all he wanted to do was to pull those cheeks, but she'd get annoyed. She tied her hair up and approached him.

"Griffith!"

"Ernaline."

"I didn't know you'd come back… I thought it was the one-time thing," she said, hugging him.

"Yeah, I, um… it almost was. I begged my mum enough to sneak me out of the citadel and bring me here again. She prefers Allen to take care of me in a faraway place where she can't see me."

"So… are you going to leave soon?" she asked.

"I don't know, but I think I will have to. My father… not Allen, I mean Lord Rosendale. He'd be suspicious if I disappeared for too long."

Ernaline sighed. "This might very well be our last meeting, but I do love you, baby boy."

Griffith blushed, frantically shaking his head. "I am going to be eleven — don't call me that — and then be just two years younger than you."

"I know."

Silence encompassed these children, two of the many innocent victims of an unfortunate fate.

"Erna?" he finally spoke. "Where do you come from?"

"From somewhere, where your father cannot return, because he chose to be with your mother. Much like you, I get to be here… because he happens to be the only trustworthy way for my people to temporarily see the world."

"Then can you take me to where you live, please?"

She shook her head, this time with a solemn expression. "No. If I take you there, it will be the end of us."

Griffith choked up at this point. "But I… But I…"

"I know. I feel the same. Pretty boy."

Bling

He was awakened from the dream when the train came to a stop. He quickly wrapped his hair up and put on his oversized cap. He rubbed the sleep away from his eyes and walked towards the gates. The station was already flooded with people, but he managed to make his way out.

"Psh!" he said to himself. "Promises, huh?"

A cursed gift

Knock

"Come in," called Jack.

The lock clicked open, followed by a muffled creak, and Van Vuren stepped in. He had a cloth bag in one hand, which Jack assumed contained some food. He carefully placed it on Jack's work table facing the window which overlooked the city. Despite the weight of it, he put it down as gentle as a feather.

Van Vuren sighed and leaned against the doorframe. His etiquette was slightly less immaculate than usual; with the sleeves of his white shirt creased up, and the khaki waistcoat slightly out of alignment. Jack knew that whatever Van was experiencing was probably more stressful than what he felt.

"Jack, you didn't come to eat... Are you feeling all right?" asked Van Vuren in a fatherly concerned manner.

"I don't know," said Jack, still peering through the window. His eyes were wide open, but they strained from the lack of sleep. "The priest... the prophecy... I never realised this place had its own box of nutcases."

Van Vuren sighed. "It is what it is. They all thought that they saw a sickle, one of Grim's apprentices, that day."

Jack shook his head. "The sickle, huh?"

"You can be assured that the guilt does not lie on you," Van told him. Somehow, Jack doubted the confidence that was in Van's half-confident reassurance.

"I don't know. Was it just a coincidence, or was it the fact that you wanted to see that happen?"

Van did not respond, as if realising it was almost better to let him feel what he did for the time. Jack kept gazing over the horizon, his hands steepled in front of him on the table.

Jack swore. "Seems like wherever I step in, only the bad things happen." He got up and walked out of the door as Van Vuren made way for him. He had a narrow cobblestone path in his garden, with oak and maple trees on either side, with some cherry bushes. He made his way towards the black iron gate, which reached to his chin. Van Vuren had closed it on his way, so he undid the clasp and walked out.

He walked down the hill, taking in the nebulous purple evening shade over the city. It had been three days since the incident, but it had not been kind on him. The pastors, the whisper-mongers, the public, the supporters, and the fear-mongers alike would not stop discussing it. He hadn't been out since then, or to near neighbourhoods or schools, simply because he was afraid of being recognised. Truth be told, most people were elated to see that sighting, but from the monster's own eye, he felt like he was in a menagerie.

Although a couple of weeks ago he had felt like finally finding a place where he belonged, he didn't feel it any more. He didn't belong here, just as he didn't on the surface.

Making his way from the backwaters of the city to the eastern highway, he saw windows lit up, televisions booming, every now and then noises of children, adults sitting on their porch having a conversation, or grilling something for dinner. It was a quite standard thing for a Friday night, but not for someone like him, or anyone on the outside world.

As he had nothing to do, he decided to walk towards the lake. He still wasn't able to even generate ripples, let alone learn the power, so he had decided to just act like an average person. Sometimes he was tempted, wishing that the power he had that day would return, but it did not work, no matter how hard he tried.

After half an hour or so, he reached the city square. There, by the church at the corner of east highway, stood a pastor. People leaving from their shops and businesses were gathering around him. Vendors, even, were peering and poking their heads to see what the pastor had to say. Usually, this wasn't supposed to happen until Sunday, but the tone seemed urgent. Jack was now close enough to make out what the pastor said. He was perched upon the four-feet-tall boundary wall of the church made of red bricks. The boundary wall was stout but short, as the church and the foreground were actually built at underground level, with bleached stone stairs leading down to them.

"What, do you really mean it?" he heard someone shout.

"Yes, God tells me so. In my prayer, what you saw that way was no mere light show staged by the children. It is indeed the Grim incarnated through the boy."

"Ah, leave the boy alone, and let us do us. How do you know it isn't just a random power?" the voice replied.

"I swear upon Grim's grave!" proclaimed the priest, silencing the protesters. "The Grim's sickle and scythe were our weapons in the final war, and I give that the sickle has returned. It only means but one thing — another uprising!"

There were collective groans from the crowd. The pastor was promising things which were considered merely symbolic, as agreed by Van Vuren and the elders.

"No wonder you dummies were overthrown by the Sanctum; you're still reading your books and listening to an idiot for your salvation..." There was a sudden voice from a teen, wearing a black hoodie which screamed of rebellious behaviour.

The pastor went to further reply, but suddenly a brick flew past his ear. After that, discord broke into the crowd, with the believers versus the sceptics going at each other alike. Two deacons grabbed the pastor by his arms, while the other two fended him off from the crowd. One of the deacons protectively wrapped his arm around the pastor's head, and they dragged him down the stairs, back into the safety of the church. The aggression dissipated eventually and people started returning to their business. Jack shook his head. He knew he wouldn't be able to tune out this chaotic scene from his mind, especially considering that much of it had to do with him.

Regardless, he decided to run his way through the west road, where it led up the lake. Maybe he'd go fishing under the effulgence of the lighthouse, since the evening was much darker. The water would be black, except for the reflections of the city lights. It would be a state of serenity, with a cold breeze and icy vapours whipping against his face. That is what he preferred, rather than be with the group playing games.

The last block of the highway leading up the lake was basically a dirt road. It was a low-maintenance area in general, with vines growing over the cement boundary wall. It was choked bottom up from moss and algae, and the barbed wires were all rusted and fragile. Even the houses were beaten down and rustic, with the day's haul of fish resting in the giant freezers set up on their porches.

He walked through the husk of an iron gate. The lake was like a black, gaping maw, twinkling with the artificial moonlight of the cave ceiling. The surface of the lake seemed a bit restless today with the wind, as the cavern was enormous enough to have some sort of atmosphere of its own. That was, of course, also true only because of the artificial weather system the Dark had. If he looked up, he could see the ripples at the ceiling and around the far walls, slightly yellowish and very much like an aurora. He didn't understand how that worked, but looking up at the barely visible peaks of the giant stalactites in the cavern ceiling, covered by the swirling ripples, he was left amazed.

He walked to his right, towards the boats and canoes floating at the dock. As he walked, there was a boulder near the shore, curving inwards so he couldn't see its side which faced the river. When he got nearer, he was surprised to see the tall, towering figure of Lex. He was clad in his usual denim bib and a worn-out grey T-shirt clinging barely on his frame. Jack never thought he'd see this big fellow standing against a boulder, introspective while watching a river.

Jack approached him warily. Lex had placed some pebbles on the top of the boulder, which he was picking up and splashing across the river. Although the boulder barely reached above Lex's chest, it dwarfed Jack completely, reaching slightly over his head. Lex didn't notice him approaching; his chin was up, and his eyes were distant, sort of with a morose expression, perhaps.

"Hey, man. Uh… didn't think you would be here," said Lex, nodding in acknowledgement of Jack's presence; but he did not make any eye contact. Instead, he randomly picked one of the pebbles resting on the boulder and chucked it into the river with a lazy arc.

"Here for the same reason as you."

"Ah, right," Lex replied, before pausing. "I am… I didn't mean to hurt anyone that day. I wouldn't have killed anyone. I just… I just don't know what happened. Sometimes, no matter how much you tell yourself that you don't want to care, you just want to win at something. Even if it means bringing the monster out of you in the end."

"It's all right, buddy, I get you."

"So, are you here to fish?" Lex asked. Jack nodded. "Well, all right then, there's something I can show you." Lex picked a random pebble up, smooth but shaped like a shard. He threw the pebble sharp as a slingshot, and it pierced the water and mushed through the glistening green skin of a trout lingering at the surface. He then jogged towards the river bank, the water splashing up to his knees as he waded in. He picked it by the tail and brought it back, setting it gently on the large boulder he was leaning against. The only evidence of the fish's existence left in this river was the pool of blood dissipating in the dark water.

"Well, that was that. A gentle death."

Lex nodded. "Well, there you go then."

Jack shook his head. "How?"

"I mean… the same way you beat me."

Jack laughed. "I don't have it. I didn't even know I had it during the moment."

Lex pursed his lips. "Ah, well… also don't be guilty about my detention. If there was any way to end the last year of school, this was the right way for me."

Jack nodded, finding the appropriate moment to talk with Lex about this. "You are from the Smithson clan, aren't you?"

Lex looked momentarily surprised. "Ah, yes I am. What gives, though?"

"Nothing. I was reading up, and found out that your family history is known to have the strongest people in the Dark."

Lex looked utterly surprised. "You kind of scare me, man. I think you should go get some sleep."

Jack grinned. "Well, true. I guess its best that I head off, then," he said, and walked away, feeling lucky about the piece of puzzle which he'd recently discovered.

Frustration

Right hook, left cross, uppercut. Bob and weave. Right hook, left cross, uppercut, side step.

No! Wrong combination. Again. Right hook, left jab… No. Again.

UGH! she thought to herself. It wasn't working. Nothing was working. The combinations weren't fluid, or natural. They were not simultaneous, but slow and disorganised. To attack was to let the body seamlessly flow through movement, without interference of thought. Where the thought came, the body would lose its own instinct. Fighting could merely be an altercation, to protect oneself or pulverise another; but to treat it as an art, like she did, made it a whole different pursuit.

She kicked the heavy bag once more, and let it ricochet against the wall behind it. She walked out of the small chamber containing the heavy bags, and into the common room, which was separated from the chamber with two black pillars in between. The entire common room was built with black tiles, with a massive screen and a snug set-up of enormous, plushy recliners and couches to view the holographic TV or just lay around.

Her friends were deeply engrossed in a game, screaming and hollering in excitement at having a go at the controllers. Here, the traditions were always old school. Despite having fully functioning VR rooms, with realistic simulations, they preferred to play on-screen rather than being taken to a pseudo-realistic simulation.

No one could sense her agitation, despite her aggressive training in the back. It annoyed her further. She approached the couch where the twins Zack and Ferrell sat, each of them holding a controller. Maverick also held one. Lappy had a huge bucket of popcorn, completely enraptured by the game. And there was Ashley, perching on the armrest of the couch. Bunch of nerds, she thought.

Zach lolled his head backwards to see her. "What's up? You wanna play?"

"Actually…" said Reyn, who grabbed a controller, which was being passed between Zack and Ashley, and slammed it abruptly into the glass table in front of them. Ashley's smile seemed to vanish, replaced by concern.

"You okay?"

"Can you not let us enjoy but a moment of peace just a few days into the vacations?" Maverick sneered, visibly irritated by the interruption.

"Whatever," she said, and left.

"What's going on with her?"

"Probably time of the month," said the twins.

"She'll be okay," said Ashley defensively. "Just let her be."

There were more concerns, surely, but they turned into wisps, as she made her way out of the dormitory, and then through the empty corridors of the school. During the evening, a couple of spotlights were kept open on the school ground for the students to walk through. She almost considered going back to her mother, who lived in the Europe district, within a very Irish neighbourhood. They'd sit on the little porch in the front, having a few drinks; she'd even smoke a bit, while her mother would go on a chain-smoking spree. She didn't like doing it, but it eased her up. Her mother would talk about the neighbourhood and their neighbours. About kids from other families and their job, or kids who had performed worse this year than last. She'd try to talk Reyn out of military training, insisting on how useless it was, and how she could just take the degree and continue with another job.

But she never managed to convince her, so she'd talk about some Irish history, and then move forward to rolling television shows which were pirated from the surface. She had custom-ordered an old-school flat screen, as she despised the holographic TV which represented the new world for her. During commercials, she'd often talk about how the street was silent, with most families sleeping early and staying reserved, accustomed to raising children and following their school routine. Only on weekends would she head out, but just by herself — her mother would find it awkward to fit in. Her youthful behaviour, paired with her funky haircuts and a cigarette always wedged between her fingers didn't help, either. And in the end, she'd follow up by saying how she'd like to buy or rent a house in a livelier street near the highways, where she could head out on the weekends. It never went anywhere, however: working as a clerk in a rescue shelter for animals didn't do much for them financially.

Reyn went through the routine in her head, and decided against it. It wasn't that she disliked being with her mother, but this just wasn't the night where she felt like being there. The lives of people, the way of the city, the debates raging in the bars, with men discussing the state of political affairs of the outside world as if they knew any better, the mundane life people lived, pretending that living in this large rock was normal. It was all beyond her. For someone who wasn't finicky, she couldn't describe how bored she felt thinking of all of it.

It was as if the way she viewed her world now was focused on a much bigger area than this tiny cavern. The thought process had no longer been concerned with the cull de sac she grew up in, but with what could be possible outside. In a world which she never knew, but knew it existed.

She remembered going to her father's bakery. It was in the middle of a crowded street, but very homely, warm and aromatic. She could practically smell the cigar in the atmosphere, mixed with the aroma of the confectionery, just by thinking about it. Her father would smudge the cigar off on the ashtray kept on the countertop before she'd arrive. That was a while ago, however; she wasn't even old enough to understand when he had passed away from a stroke. Her family tree in the Dark wasn't really known to have many power users, either. She only found hers while roaming lost as a child and almost being hit by a car. It was then that a miraculous defence barrier sprang up and saved her. The rest was history, and she was enrolled personally by Van Vuren in the military school. She considered visiting the area with that bakery once again, but she knew it was long gone. It was sold long ago in order to repay the debts which her mother couldn't manage.

Speaking of places to go, however, she looked in the direction of the Eastern hills, where Jack had bought a house, right beside Van Vuren's hill. He really is the cause of this frustration, she thought. Thinking of a foreign guy who'd been rescued at the cost of the security of the entire place, only for him to purchase a house and sulk away in it. It had only been three days since the event, but it wasn't like he couldn't show up to their group at least. He'd even lost his phone, or that was his excuse for never responding. She understood where her irritation stemmed from. As a bird with a fluttering heart, trying to leave the cave, she couldn't let the one who'd promised her to slip away like that.

She reached the hill in a short while and climbed up, undoing the clasp on the iron gate and then walking through his garden. At least this is well kept, she thought, reaching the ebony door and then knocking.

"Come in," a voice came from inside.

Oh, so he's alive at least.

She parted the door halfway through and glanced inside. There he was, slouched on a black chair with a controller loosely held in his hands. One of his legs rested on the floor, the foot clad in a torn sock, and the other resting on a small table. Just looking at his posture made her feel pain in her lumbar region. His coat was draped on the back of his chair, and he wore just a plain white shirt.

"Hey, Reyn."

"Hi..."

"How have you been?"

"I am fine. You?"

"Not at all, will you cut the crap?

"Ah, all right. I... uh, finished this game."

"Yeah?"

"Humph. It's this game about a father and a daughter surviving through a zombie apocalypse."

"Right. I am familiar with that."

"I liked the feeling of being a parent. It's interesting, though, that back then people almost fantasised about getting to watch the world end."

She understood where he was trying to go. "It's crazy. Maybe it's like a way of reminding yourself what the world can become if you don't do anything to change it," she said. "But even then, they preserved relationships in these stories. As if to say that without family, or someone to love, it would be purposeless to survive."

"It sure is."

Now she had to say why she was there. "Jack. It's been three days since you've talked to anyone. To any one of us. Hell — you've lost your phone. How will you contact your friend on the surface when you return? I am sorry for the whole disaster, and about the people here acting crazy, but you've got to move on." She paused for a moment, gathering her thoughts. "I don't want to see you get attached to this cavern and rot here forever. I know it seems like I am pushing you just for my wishes, but no. I hate that people get stuck in this little world here, and I can't see you be one of them. There's no purpose here, and I hope that you see that."

He went silent, with a sombre expression. Had she spoken too much? Had she come across as forceful? She didn't know, but she hoped that her concerns hadn't come across as abrasive remarks. She was on the verge of apologising and walking away, when he finally spoke.

"Well, I understand..." He sat up, fixing his posture and immediately losing the languidness. He then bent forward and placed the controller gently back on the table beside the monitor. The top of the table was a mess as well, riddled with papers and books. He then let his hand slowly glide across the table, his brow furrowing in concentration for which paper to pick. He stopped, ruffled a particular jumble of notes, and picked out one. He then sat back and, with a gesture, beckoned her to sit.

"You're right, I shouldn't have just silently holed myself up. But I had been doing more than feeling sorry for myself."

Reyn felt an urge to apologise, but he waved it away.

"I just lack resources. If I tell you everything, will you help me with what I need?"

"Yes! I'd be glad... glad to be of any assistance!" She felt a rush: this is actually happening.

"So, uh, bear with me. This is going to get nuts. You know the knight Griffith Rosendale, the Arch..."

"Of course I do. I was crazily charmed by him."

Jack laughed, shaking his head. Reyn blushed. "Hey, I was naïve, you know?"

"But anyway," he continued, "and one of your horsemen, Ernaline Tora?"

"What about her?"

"They might've really known each other."

Reyn gaped at him with eyes as wide as an owl.

"What do you mean? How do you know?"

"I may have broken in and dug up records from your military school. The archives even had a basement which went back to the place where people of the Dark lived even before this cave was found. And well, I realised that she studied at the University of Eastern Massachusetts."

"And?"

He picked up a knife and threw it like a bolt; it wedged into the knight's picture on his wall. "And well, I happen to be aware of the background of the knight; he, too, had studied in that university. They both enrolled and completed their education around the same time."

"So?" she asked, still not getting his point. "It could be a coincidence. She must've used a fake identity. In that case, you can't expect Griffith to have found her, right? I don't think people of even their prowess and stature can find each other just like that."

"Exactly, it could be a coincidence. But guess what? This goes a decade back now. Apparently, a general from the Smithson clan was excommunicated from the Dark for something he did; but during summers the Dark would still let some of their children go to his farm as a part of their summer trip. These trips included Ernaline as well."

Reyn nodded, incredulous. “Okay, so a general was excommunicated from the Smithson clan; but we still trusted him?”

“Yes… being of the Smithson clan also meant that the general must have possessed amazing strength. Does this remind you of someone in the Sanctum?”

Reyn gasped in surprise, as everything sank into place. “Knight Griffith has that power. It means that somehow the excommunicated general is related to him. Meanwhile, Ernaline got to visit this general’s place as a kid. This means they might have gotten to know each other long before the university!”

“Yes!” Jack cried in affirmation. “All I have to do is test this theory.”

Reyn shook her head, still surprised. “If this is true, then it is something which not even Van Vuren and the elders would know.”

“No,” said Jack. “Van Vuren obviously knows who the excommunicated general is, and maybe some other stuff. But it looks like the elders are trying to hide some of the history which took place before this cave was built.”

“But why would they do that?”

Jack shook his head. “I have no idea. But anyways, I’ll have to make a trip to this university and find their records. If all of this is true, it may start untangling this whole knot.”

“All right, then… so be it. I guess I will get you whatever you need; but you’ve got to come with me.”

"Let's get going," said Jack, getting up from his chair and stretching.

"Hey, Jack, wait..." she said, licking her lips. There was still some business remaining. "Have you ever — uh, do you wanna arm wrestle?"

Jack looked at her, incredulous, and then burst out laughing. She joined in, too; he kind of had a haggard but infectious laugh. As the laugh fluttered down, he eyed her bare arms and raised his eyebrows. "I am sure I can handle you."

"Oh, really? See if you can."

In one swift motion, he swept the junk off a table behind him and then set two chairs on either side of it. Each of them then took the opposite chair and prepared themselves. It was the first time that she really noticed how fit he was in his shirt.

"What are you waiting for?" he said, putting his arm on the table.

She snapped out of it, pretending that nothing had happened, and then braced her hand against his. "Sorry if I am sweaty; I was training before coming here."

"Nah, don't worry; you really smell nice, actually."

Reyn flushed up pink, not having a response to that. He counted down from three, and then it began. They both started chuckling, and then laughing while they were at it, looking at each other's expression as they exerted force. He was definitely harder than she thought, his muscles tensed up in the action. With a few false flags and near-wins, she finally put in her last ounce of power, and his hand hit the table with a thud. She smiled broadly, and then cheered, before they got up and left his home for the trip.

Right up your alley

The music cut through the corner, only faintly at first, but getting bold as they approached an adjoining alley, perpendicular to the one which they were in. The alley was gated and restricted on both sides, only meant for the people who meant business. Jack didn't know what the business was yet, but he already had the inkling all right.

As soon as they entered the adjoining alley, the music blasted, riffing off the walls. The alley itself was more like a street, sandwiched between wide, three-storey buildings, and was closed off by a massive wall on the opposite end. The only way to enter was by the one they had just come from.

Jack swore undcr his breath, walking behind Reyn, taking it all in. It was a heaven for the amorous. Even as they walked, a couple passed by them, with the girl brash like a demon, grappling her mate closely. She pushed her across the street, until her mate was back-first into the mortar-oozing wall. She had raven-black hair sweeping across her face, and her eyes were heavily doused in eye-liner. She bared her teeth as she had her way with her mate, who was whimpering against the wall.

Jack averted his gaze, but the flagrancy wasn't done yet; in fact, this is what this place was. Everywhere he looked, there were people engaged in trysts. Even as they passed a flattened junk car, squatting beside a pavement in front of what seemed to be an entrance, with rolled-up shutters leading into the place, a couple of guys went at it on the bonnet of a car. This was just two of the cases; the rest just inundated the scene to a point where Jack just got over it.

When they finally stepped up to the first entrance with a rolled-up shutter, he saw the place in its entirety. It was a club, raging with strobe lights, purple and green and pink. The place was consternating: it didn't seem to have much security, and he didn't know why Reyn had specifically chosen it. They stood there for a few seconds, with Reyn contemplating which way to go. She squinted, eyeing a staircase at the right corner of the club, only obscurely visible in the dizzying lights. A couple of men passed by, eyeing Reyn depravedly. "Jeez, what a walking treat!", "You reckon we can drug her out and knock her upstairs?"

Jack spun around in a blind rage. Reyn hadn't heard them, as she had approached a girl, smoking away at the bar, to ask about something; but he had stood right there, at the summit of the entrance. Before he could act, however, he felt his overcoat sleeve being tugged, and then he was being dragged along by Reyn, towards the same stairwell she'd been peering at.

"Reyn, uh, those guys right there..."

"What?"

"Yeah, they were really saying horrible..."

"No, I mean I can't hear you!" she yelled, in order to be heard. Jack tried to shout back, but him shouting did nothing but make him lose his voice.

She dragged him up the staircase, and then he spoke again, as the music was slightly tuned out.

"Reyn, those guys, those guys I swear really had a messed-up idea going on in their heads."

"Ah, shit happens; you ignored them, right?"

"No, I was mad — but you caught me."

"That's good. If you and I were to knock out every disgusting person there is, we'd end up in a blind world." She resumed walking down the corridor, where another staircase led them up.

He followed her silently, having not much to say after what she had said. The plywood-floored corridor shook, vibrating with the beats. The walls were minimally adorned with pale green wallpaper with flowery patterns. It was like walking through a cheap motel.

When they reached the spiralling staircase made of stone with a wooden balustrade, Reyn spoke.

"Okay, Jack, Tommy can be tedious to deal with. Try to be subtle. He can be a sissy if you act up, or try to play games on you. Don't buy into whatever he says."

"Okay. How do you know all that about him and this place, though?"

"Well, let's say I wasn't the smartest girl a few years back. He's a few years older than me, but it's an experience which I would be pleased to avoid ever again."

Jack smiled, looking sideways. "Well, all right, I understand."

Reyn blushed, and then grunted, "You'd better not see into it more than what it is."

"Okay, okay, I get it."

They reached the room, which was, as led by the stairwell, constructed on the roof of the building, only lit by a dim, yellowish bulb hanging by a wire. The walls were white and oil-painted. It seemed like a storeroom, if anything. She knocked. "Hey, Tommy?"

It stayed silent for half a moment, followed by a stern voice. "Cut!" Then, with a raucous cheer, mainly comprising of girls, the door burst open and a gaggle of girls wearing deep blue crop tops and skirts rushed out. They went by, cheering and giggling. It was bewildering, but no more so than the yellow crescent moon and star pattern on their dresses, as if pulled out straight from a cartoon.

Within the room there was a single bed, a TV in front, and a bald, pot-bellied, haggard-looking cameraman, clad in a black waistcoat and denims, packing up his camera equipment. Tommy, though, their subject, was on a king-sized bed, the sheets and pillows covered in the same cartoonish moon and star pattern. He sat there naked, or at least half-covered up to the waist by the ridiculous sheet. He had curly auburn hair, on both the head and chest. He looked at Jack with dreamy green eyes and an unusual interest.

"Hey, girl, been so long. So what brings you here?" he said in a tone as if addressing someone close to him.

"Shut it. We just need some…"

"Help, yes? No wonder you're here. Who else remembers me from the school? Poor me," he replied in mock innocence.

"Look, nobody's gonna come to this banged-up place, with a business that you're licensed for," Reyn spat, already annoyed by him. They instantly went into a staring contest of who crumbled first. Reyn looked ferocious, but just as hilarious trying to maintain it. Jack couldn't tell which stood out more for him.

Tommy gave way, pretending to wave it off. "Okay, okay, whatever. Say what you need. But it won't be free; as you see, my business runs on the exchange of services." He winked. Reyn half-glanced at Jack awkwardly. "Well, that sounds awkward. I mean, pay me up and I shall serve what you need."

"That is an interesting choice of business you made," Jack chimed in suddenly.

Reyn frowned at him.

"Well, yeah, thanks. See Reyn? This guy gets me."

"So you were a prodigy?"

"Hell yeah, back at college."

"Well then?" said Jack, gazing around at the inexplicably raunchy bedroom set-up.

"Oh, this is the place where the magic happens. You lookin' at that camera, right?"

"Interesting."

"You bet."

"Guys, back to topic," Reyn intervened impatiently. "Actually, close your security cameras."

"They're all off, honey," assured Tommy, his hand slightly slithering under the sheets.

"And your phone, too."

"Uh, there's no phone..."

Reyn raised her hand slightly, and surely, and the phone blew out of the sheet, smashing into the window sill on the wall opposite to them. Tommy quickly gathered up the sheet to hide his bushy auburn interior.

"Damn, when did you learn telepathy? Powers don't work like tha..."

"Remember, dummy, my power is defence. It means it will literally defend me from anything, even if it is just a phone innocently recording me against my will," she said, sneering at him. "And anyway, we want weapons. Not old-school, bullet-firing ones. A couple of lightning-discharge guns and wave blasters, maybe a disintegrating baton."

Tommy blew a raspberry, followed by an invisible slap which rocked his head backwards. Jack saw Reyn in amazement: she really was going in for those weapons. Lightning-discharge guns could quite literally discharge voltages at the maximum of one billion volts; akin to a ferocious bolt striking the land from the sky. The wave blasters, in common colloquial, meant weapons that emitted microwave radiation that, in a given parameter, could fry someone's brains out. Needless to say, they were used by Sanctum military, but also copied by the Dark for combat.

After a considerable amount of pausing, Tommy replied, "I can't. It is not possible. You know, I could dish out a dozen rifles if you'd ask, in exchange for jack shit pretty much. But this, you could take my left testicle a hostage and I'd still back down from this."

"A thousand Revols, Tommy," said Reyn, attempting to subdue him.

He raised his eyebrows. "Well, I am interested, but it'd take more than just piquing my interest."

Reyn groaned. It was what she probably thought was sufficient. But Tommy was more than a brothel-runner. He produced movies, regulated escorts, probably regulated drugs and everything bad this city dealt with. Jack had an inkling of how to pay him up, and with an educated guess, he was going to hold Tommy a hostage for something more than just his left testicle.

"Here," said Jack, and he pulled his phone out, punching in his code and opening up his account. "Take whatever you need, but get the work done."

Tommy scowled, not having expected this. And then he chuckled nervously as he took the phone. "I mean… fair enough; but these weapons you ask for… you guys better know the level of crime which you're getting into."

"You see that villa beside the Eastern Hills? That belongs to…"

"Shove your villa where the sun doesn't shine. I know you're the rich guy, the guy from the surface. Now I realise, I've heard all about you. Van Vuren risked our good men to rescue the likes of you, and now you're using this poor girl for your own benefit."

"Don't pretend you give a crap about this place. You're corrupting the people here."

"Oh, yeah? Well, you don't know about that. Anyway, I manage the warehouse, and I plan to stay loyal to the military. If you both don't leave now, I plan to use this confrontation as evidence for your attempted crime."

Reyn tried to intervene to break the tension, but Jack held up his hand, smiling.

"Sure, Tommy. You want me to tell the military about the drugs you import from the Scythe? Or how you might have questionable standards of what counts as the legal age to be involved in your movies?"

"That is false!" cried Tommy. He lunged from his position to grab the pistol resting on the table beside his bed; but with a swift roundhouse kick, fast as lightning, Reyn had knocked him out.

"Pft, what a disgrace," muttered Reyn, rubbing her ankle; she had hit the decorative metal framework on the bed. "Well, anyway... Jack, about the things which you said: how do you know?"

"Well, I said the drug thing because I had heard of the guy from the junkies at the school, and assumed that this guy was it. As for the other thing, that was only a blank threat."

"Jesus!" whispered Reyn, and she climbed across the bed to get to the cabinet and found the keys. Tommy had rolled on the floor, butt-naked and tangled in his ridiculous moon-and-stars sheet. "I am disappointed that a place like this gets no quality checks."

"Well, from what I know, people usually do not like authorities fiddling with their pleasure places."

"All right then, let's get the guns, and we will then get the device you need from Lappy."

"Okay, but if Tommy speaks up?"

"He won't. I'll make sure. If he does, he will also risk having this place shut down."

"Okay."

"And listen, Jack," said Reyn, smiling earnestly. "Our people here often talk about fixing the world above, but thank you for fixing the mess that we have down here."

An old friend's plight

Alex woke up at the break of noon with a mild throbbing in his temples. His eyes felt as if they were being dragged down by a sledge, or at least that's what the dreadful sensation felt like. It was beyond grogginess, and almost like a terrible hangover. He sprang up from his bed — no tottering morning rituals or stretching or yawning. He had slept in jeans, a white T-shirt and a red and black-striped flannel. He still had his black leather wrist watch; he touched the screen, seeing 12:05PM appear with a sun and palm tree in the background.

He gazed at his single-mattress bed for the last time with his favourite, threadbare sheet with now-fading quatrefoil pattern adorned with flowery designs, lit dimly by the light seeping through the light blue curtain, which the bed was horizontally placed against. He eyed the small ebony cabinets squatting at either side of his bed, placed with dirty white lamps. The only thing he really hated to leave was the guitar resting beside his cupboard; the one which had made him the high school sweetheart in the days when he had dreamed of being a musician and skipped classes, perfecting the frets for the notes he wrote himself.

He sighed and went off to the kitchen to brew himself a quick coffee from the machine, filling his large cream-coloured mug, and went to his bedroom again. The coffee didn't sit well today with his lack of appetite, but he decided to sip through regardless. He grabbed his backpack and swung it over his shoulder, scoured through his drawers and found his belongings, perfuming himself with a flowery, sickly-sweet scent he found. Not the best, but it was all he had. He grabbed his keys and prepared to walk out of the apartment, wishing to never return again. Before he left, however, something was nagging, something that he was forgetting. With a quick realisation, he went and grabbed his phone that he'd placed in the tiny gap that was between the boundary of the bed frame and his mattress.

He checked his messages once again — ninety-one in total — which he didn't care about. One in particular, being unresponsive for almost a month now, was the chat log with Jack. After Jack's abduction, he had sent about three messages.

What's up, dude, it's been 5 minutes but I hope you're fine — the message was seen minutes later.

So it's been a day, what you up to? Message was unseen, but Jack was online momentarily.

Hey man, I hope all's fine, and you aren't chopped into minced meat yet, right? Followed up by: *Sorry that was a bad joke, I am just nervous.*

And that had been it. He'd never been online again to see or respond; his identification chip code had gone offline, so Alex couldn't access him through Common Registry. Either. He clicked on Jack's profile picture, to see him grinning broadly towards the sea at Orient beach on their trip, his hair wildly swept over by the wind. For some uncertain feeling, Alex's hand shook, in anger or nervousness, he didn't know, but he wanted to delete this contact and forget it forever, but he couldn't bring himself to do it.

He stuffed the phone aggressively in his jeans pocket and then strode to his door, abruptly leaving after locking the door. His departure time for New Orleans was at 1.30pm, an hour's walk from his place — but he was fine with it. He felt glum, not in a tearful way, but in a way that was a realisation of being a walking spectre, of loneliness that came from social detachment. Self-fulfilment through friends and family would have been everything two years ago, and had you told him he'd be a sulking nobody, he'd have laughed it off. But it was clearly not the case anymore. His passion for music had dropped inevitably after the struggle to find a college, which he'd decided to leave and join the military instead. Knowing everything as he did now, he just did not find the energy in him to spend five years to be washed into a helmeted, silenced soldier.

Sometimes, he wished he had re-entered college, but going back was like an ultimate shame in the boarding, and he wasn't inclined enough in his conviction to do so. He was going back to his loving family, which thankfully was wealthy, running an independent line of small businesses. Maybe the love of his four siblings and his parents and his warm, snug room would restore him; if he accepted his loss of grandeur and music career after his abysmal state of denial. Either way, he kept trudging through the highly crowded sidewalks of New York, nearing Penn station.

A chill breeze passed by. He felt his otherwise secure jeans pocket a little awkward against his thigh, as if it was touched, so he decided to check it. The inner fabric felt slightly pulled out, but everything was fine. His cards, his tickets, even his phone — all fine. He decided to momentarily stop and recheck his backpack, see if his documents and clothes were still there. Everything seemed okay, but rather… something? Either way, he wasn't paranoid, so he swung his backpack onto his shoulders again. Another chill breeze passed by, plastering his bangs across his eyes. He swept them away angrily with his fingers and his vision cleared: a hunched figure was crossing the pedestrians' path in front of him. He decided to keep walking; the sky had turned surprisingly overcast, with shivering breeze.

"What troubles you?" A breeze? No, a rustling whisper called him.

Alex looked at the hunched figure again. "Nothing. Why do you ask?"

"Heh, heh, just a surprisingly lazy day to be fretting alone."

"I am not fretting — and lazy? What… do you mean by it?" His voice faltered, realising the road had completely become free of traffic; but also, were the pavements… empty? Where did the people go? "Anyway, good day to you," he said, starting to walk again.

"Where are you going?"

Alex swung backwards, irritated. "Will you stop and get lost, you freak?"

The figure seemed no more than an anorexic boy, maybe of his age, but heinously hunched, his hands behind his back. One arm came forth, and then the other, unnaturally thin and long; and, like strange contortions, he spread his arms, gesturing at the apparently empty surroundings. "This road isn't empty; it is just devoid of people who understand you."

"What do you mean?" Alex slowly navigated his hand towards his jeans pocket, to his phone, but his hands had started to shake and he couldn't grip it.

"I mean precisely as I say, and you know it. It is empty; no one understands you. But then why am I here?" He pointed at the buildings, his face uncannily looking up and following the motion of his hands. "But these are empty, as empty as your soul. Your knowledge empties you. You want to burn your friend down; for he left after all that you did for him. Why run from it?"

Alex flushed. "No, I don't. We all feel that when we're hurt, but not like that."

"But he's gone; gone where he doesn't care for you."

"What do you even know about it?"

Alex felt his soul nearly jump out of his body when the man looked directly at him, and Alex gazed into two bottomless pits inside the eye sockets. He broke his eye contact away; he was frantic and winded out. He felt uneasy, but he had to look up. Perspiration ran down his body, but he had to stand his ground. He stared back at a sickly pale face and sunken eyes, eerie but ashamedly not what he should have been terrified of.

"Say what you have to..." muttered Alex, realising that there were people walking by again... and the traffic was back. *What?* he thought, glancing at the man for explanation.

He could not look away; he was locked. The man's arms went behind his back once again, and his hunch returned to its grotesque level.

"Come with me, and let me tell you about this concrete of ashes you stand upon. These whitewashed walls. Bleeding mothers. Weeping soldiers. A resurrected god."

A forbidden friendship

The lavatory light blinked on, dimly bathing the surroundings in a yellowish hue. Jack bent over the cream-coloured basin and splashed the cold water across his face again and again, a habit of his which he'd repeat until his skin would be dry.

He looked in the mirror; the dim lighting was perhaps too grim, giving him harsh features. His sunken stone-grey eyes and cheekbones especially looked prominent, giving him a wolfish visage. Again and again, he splashed, facing the mirror, but he didn't stare at himself. His thoughts were beyond the motion; or, in fact, back in time. Memories which had dissolved into mist during his recent years came flooding back through a dream this morning. Long before he had his big break with the work that he'd gotten by solving cases, he was scurrying in the halls of a public Sanctum school.

Clunk.

He panted heavily as he crashed into the locker. He fidgeted for the key, shaking as he unlocked the locker. Inside, he had nothing; there were no holographic devices, and no touch pads either which were specifically designed for different subjects. The only things left were his anxiety medicines. He shoved them in his mouth by the fistful, and then slumped against the locker door. He was hyperventilating; there was nothing to do but fail. He was a lost child; a name designated to children who never left the boarding school because they didn't have a family to see in the summer.

He had just seen his subject pads being stolen by a bunch of fellow freshmen. They were led by the guy who loathed Jack for having been reported for stealing. He'd invite his friends over during lunch every single day, and, in the most non-physical way possible, lambasted and bullied Jack. It was then he wished that he hadn't acted like a nosy kid, getting into someone else's mess.

For a lost child who hermetically grew up within the restrictions of the boarding, and having his confidence systematically beaten out of him for months, he had practically become socially inept. His anxiety riddled his every pore. He could not even practically throw an apple core in a bin, even if he wanted to rid himself of it like a plague. He could not shuffle on his seat in a class; because a simple movement debilitated him. He thought of every possible scenario — a confrontation, the gazes, the silent judgment — everything that could possibly happen in those trivial, perhaps most insignificant actions. And the fact that he realised how every single one of those insecurities were meek and pointless to ponder just added another crack in the glass wall from where he viewed his insignificance.

Eventually, his erratic breathing slowed down, but the regrets pierced in regarding every single thing he'd done the day before. He'd made the mistake of telling one of his friends that he was going to report the bully again, only for the bully to have overheard it. It must be why the bully, as his punishment, took all his subject pads and drowned them in water.

He felt naked and vulnerable. If only he had managed to tell this to his teachers, they'd no doubt inspect the situation and reprimand the bully. No injustice went unpunished in the Sanctum world. However, he couldn't do it. He wouldn't be able to outlive the silent, mean looks that he'd get from anyone who had been acquainted with the bully and disapproved of Jack's action. And he knew well that it was all about the slights. No one could record slights and the judging eyes that dug daggers.

He was terrified, and, without his pads, all his work was lost. Was he going to be a failure and repeat a year when previously he'd been proud for being able to skip four grades? Was he anything if not just an able tool good at remembering and regurgitating things in the class? Was he truly intelligent if he could not oust a bunch of bullies?

But that wasn't the end of it, of course. A newcomer from the town of New Orleans, a senior and a musician, happened to stumble across him in the corridor. The rest was history. Alex helped Jack find his courage, and to do what it took to get over the torment.

"Agh!" he screamed in the highest pitch possible, as a roach ran down his hair and onto his shoulder. He jumped with such intensity that his hand nearly broke with an inadvertent smack against the door frame while he was launched into a backwards trajectory. He shook his hand in pain, sweating profusely. Of course, it had to be his mortal enemy. Had anyone been so scared that upon sighting their enemy — and in this case, a cockroach — they were launched into the air by fear and almost broke one of their bones?

Talk about a dramatic tale of good vs evil, and in the end, we still have these dumb roaches around, he thought. Either way, the little cretin innocently fell on the floor and roached his merry way to the slight crack in the grate behind the basin.

When the commotion was over, he finally wiped his face with a towel, and confronted the guilt which he had been stifling, especially after the dream. It was like his dream-self had returned once again, only to berate him for the things which he guiltily forgot. In this case, it was Alex. Reyn had provided him an alternate, encrypted phone, for him to contact Alex while he was outside. He had checked Alex's last position, and he had supposedly returned to his family house. Once Jack had finished his trip to the university, he'd immediately follow up with Alex, just to fulfil his promise at least, and to apologise for not being able to reply.

He left the motel heading out to the university. He could have been back in New York by now, but the security was too strict at night to trespass into the university, so he decided it was better off passing his way through the morning by blending into the crowd. It was like what Van Vuren once jokingly said, "You go in the night, get captured, step on contraptions, and be distraught as all the doors are locked. Go during the day, the staff shows you the way, and you get your hay."

He was on the road which led up to the university now. The beautiful spring greenery around the university was bathed in the morning sunlight, while the elegant blue entablature gracing the gate and the whitewashed boundary walls perfected the contrast. The Sanctum flag waved merrily over the gate, this time giving him a different perspective than what he'd have thought seeing it before. But even so, despite how a Sanctum university repulsed him, he had to go inside and hopefully scrounge the missing vial to finish his concoction.

He carefully eased one of the straps off his shoulder and unzipped the chains on the bag. It was time for him to test the device, to see the nifty work of the Dark itself. It was a hefty grey device with a slanting analogous display, shaped like a book wider than his hand. He glanced around quickly to check if no one had noticed, and pressed the button he was told to on the display. With an almost inaudible, high-pitched sound, it came to life, the green blinking light showing that it was working. Its purpose was simple: to create a faux connection with the Common Registry, just as if he was a citizen with a designated tracking chip with an identification number in his neck.

His own chip had stopped working due to the cave system, or the magical ripples of the place, or whatever, so he had to resort to this. He placed the device in his backpack again, strapped up, and trudged towards the steps leading up to the university. It was not like he did not have faith in the Dark's device, as he'd clearly seen it work in the case of Brock being a spy, or the members of different resistances using it to travel — it was just that being him in that position alone absolutely unnerved him.

It was also absolutely unnerving to pretend that the guards beneath those lifeless visors wouldn't just melt their way through him with their batons, had he been singled out from the swathe of students. Thankfully, amidst the rush, he made his way through. Almost. Only when he had reached the gate did a guard take particular interest in him, tilting his head. Jack did his best to appear inconspicuous and strode forward blissfully; however, the guard ominously stepped towards him. Slow steps, one after another, pretending to be as much of a hardass as he could. He stopped a step away from Jack, so Jack had to turn towards him. The guard was almost a head taller, and ran his gaze from top to bottom. Yeah, I understand, buddy, Jack thought to himself; a guy with a wide-brimmed hat, an overcoat, a shirt and a tie, hair that flowed with the wind, didn't really do well when it came to meshing with the crowd of students.

He had to think of something quick; he knew the guard was going to ask for his phone or his Common Registry device.

Suddenly, he just did that: he pulled his defunct Common Registry device out, shaped like a phone and the size of his palm. "Here, you have it… I didn't wash my hands this morning, though, you know?" And then he awkwardly winked. The guard stood there for a second, and despite the opaque visor, Jack could sense his disgust. He shook his head and turned around, walking back to his assumed position. The black tights stretching across his buttocks, coupled with the white armoured parts of his exoskeleton leg piece made his hardass march even funnier to view from the rear.

Jack walked through, and instantly strode off to wherever it would be likely to find the archives. He noticed that the students swarming in the park, cafeteria and basically everywhere in the local vicinity, were all particularly clad in white T-shirts that said "The parade reaches 17 February, be ready for the Paragon!" and he realised that the parade had been reaching to England; it must be there right now. He had forgotten to keep track of the parade and the murder and the crumpled paper he'd found. Too much was going off at different tangents; at least this was something he could confirm, and he really hoped to do so.

He stepped up to a building with red-bricked arched pillars leading into corridors with offices. This must be it, he thought, and walked towards it. It was ironic that even the university, with its penchant for a blue-and-white paint theme like the rest of the world, realised that painting over red bricks would be ridiculous.

After a few misguided strolls through the corridors and an array of awkward glances, he realised that the student profiles, and the records, may be, in fact, stored somewhere in the library archives. And so, through the wooden signboard etched into a wall, he soon found his way into the library; where, instead of a barrage of books upon the shelves like the old world, the modern libraries had a nifty system, with touchpads resting on shelves, granting individual users what would otherwise be the entire physical collection stored in a library.

All he had to do now was pick any random one, and find the application to look up what he needed. Except for the one fact: they required a Common Registry identification number confirming the presence of a student.

He looked around to make sure that no one saw his tantrum, and then banged the table with his fist.

Instead, the pain fired up from the contusion he had gotten back in the motel, and then he tripped against a chair and fell flat on his back like a snow angel. A couple of pupils threw weird looks in his direction and then hurriedly strode off.

He tapped his fingers on the floor, still perfectly imitating a snow angel, trying to think; and then he realised: he'd need to find somewhere else with an actual database of all the student profiles, and not just log into the local college library. But to see that, he'd have to begin with the darkly polished locked wooden door that loomed across the section in which he was in, with a small sign indicating 'For staff only'. Not for today, he thought, and he stood up and approached it. After traversing the distance of a couple of long tables lined with chairs, he made sure that between the two shelves, where this section was concealed within, was now only him and the door.

He took deep breaths, his fingers twitching in consternation. The door had a simple hand-scanning lock above the handle. He could either use his device or try to use the ripples for the first time. He knew they could interfere with technology, and work through an identification lock. After a couple more, deep breaths, it was time for him to use his power. He splayed his hand and examined the cool, black surface of the scanner. His plan was to place his hand on it, where it was supposed to detect his hand, and then hopefully try to make the ripples flow. It could just be that simple.

All he had to think, feel the ripples as if his hand was going through water or experiencing an intense magnetic field. He breathed deeply as he was taught, and cleared his mind, and then placed his hand in the position for scanning.

One, two, three… no response. Okay… flow, he thought in his mind, but felt a jolt go through his arm, forcing him to jump away. He checked to see if anyone saw him, but no one was there. Darn it, he thought, and resignedly pulled the device out of his bag. He wasn't sure how to make it work, but he knew if he took any longer, someone would notice him trying to trespass. Either way, he saw one of the buttons of the large device, which said, 'Identification Interception', so he pressed it, his hands slightly shaking. The device took a few moments, as a green laser shot from its front and ran down the scanner, after which the door unlocked with a click. He then sighed and turned the handle, silently stepping inside the room, hoping that he'd be able to just walk out of the place the same way.

Within the room, a row of screens was connected to a server. Their profiles could be saved into one of these. He connected the device to a server, which let him log-in, and then he searched her name in the interface. Sure enough, he saw the name which could not be missed: Ernaline Tora. On the title page were her details, along with the years that she'd studied in the university: 2292-2298. He then looked up Griffith quickly, and sure enough the dates were close, only that she had left two years earlier.

So he was right: before the second century war during which she became one of the founders of the Dark cavern, and before Griffith became a knight who vehemently played a rolc in defeating the Dark during the war, they studied in the same university. But how… how could he prove that they knew each other?

Coincidences this big do not exist, and he knew that well. He scrolled down her profile, past her dissertation, and came across her farewell letter at the end, the last paragraph of which seemed to be some glitched gibberish. He would have dismissed it, except that there was a message on the screen.

'Scanning', it said, and Jack gasped, looking at the device he had plugged into the server nearby. Had she left a message? The gibberish on the screen was then translated below in a readable paragraph:

"*Hello, my baby boy, I knew you would manage to find this. Sorry, unlike I told you, I leave before the summer ends. I was always going to finish before you... so please do not hate me. I know we planned so hard to find this opportunity to be with each other, but I realised fast that it leads to nowhere. My people need me, there is a war brewing, and as dreamy as we were... I suppose this is where our time ends. In another life, dream boy, X.*"

Jack stepped back, just contemplating what he saw. Talk about a tragic love story, huh?

Through two of the most opposite forces, forbidden by fate to ever be in that position, they had still managed to sow something. A flower which defied the confines of their destiny and bloomed in the warmth between them.

Jack exhaled through his nose, amused at finding himself in tears through this tale. Anyhow, this tale only confirmed how deep the connections went between the Dark and the Sanctum.

Make it rain

Reyn twiddled her thumbs in anticipation. Her focus was solely on her boots as she sat at the edge of her bed, fully dressed, waiting for a call. It had been an hour from his promised time, yet there were no responses, no knock on the door, nothing. She wasn't even sure that he'd have survived through the vicious security on the surface all by himself. She grimaced to think of the results of him being caught in the process.

All those flittering thoughts did little to reassure her unnerved state, to calm her firing impulses. She rechecked her phone, still devoid of any response. She inhaled deeply, shook her head and then stood up. The last thing she wanted was for herself to be an unwary person that could be duped easily.

Her eyes quickly flitted around the room until they landed on her black, polyester tactical backpack. Although it could pass as a high-end college backpack, she decided to unzip it and shift the weaponry to her jet-black backpack that she'd used for school. First, she took the lightning-discharge rifle out; it was long — longer than an average assault rifle — and noticeably heavier. It was rectangular in its body, and covered with a smooth, white insulating material. On its side was the scale of voltage that the user wanted to shoot at, which also, in fact, depended on how much power the user had. That was just for the Dark, though; for the Sanctum's version of the rifle, it had no bionic connection with the humans, since most of the time soldiers did not have power. Van Vuren would say that sometimes during battle, too much use of these weapons would kill the soldiers on their feet — something that the Dark was good at exploiting.

Either way, she took it out and stuffed it in her backpack, and then pulled the wave blasters, which looked somewhat like a normal rifle, but instead it had a much bigger barrel and on its end was a silver-coloured microwave-transmitting antenna.

She stuffed that, too, in its place, and then zipped the bag up; after which, she was on her way. She glanced through the window behind her bed for the last time, which showed her the view of the city, and then she shut and locked her dorm door. It may have been years since she'd even locked her room down, but today had come, and she wouldn't see it for a while, or a long time, perhaps.

A few rushed breaths and the shot of adrenaline made her run. She couldn't bear to walk all the way through. It was simple: she was going to make it to the four horsemen roundabout, take a left from it, exit from the lakeside gate and then break it for the cave entrance. It was more than thirty hours since he had left; sooner or later people would find out about his disappearance.

Upon rushing to the Horsemen area, and almost breaking it to the left highway, she heard her name being called out. It was the twins, she knew. She skidded to a halt, panting. She turned towards them, flipping her hair out of her vision. They were standing outside a pub that they'd all go to on weekends, wearing their matching brown sleeveless camo jackets, pink T-shirts and roughened-up denims.

"Whoa there, where are you rushing to?" asked a concerned Zachary. "Going for training or something? You can come chill with us; it is kinda peaceful here today."

"No, I…"

"Find us? Yes, we are here."

Reyn rolled her eyes. "No, you dummies. I have to go…"

"Where?"

"Outside, on the surfacc."

For a moment there was absolute silence from the dumbfounded twins, as they stared at her, jaws dropped, and the only noise was the creaking of the inn door, followed by the sound of Lappy dropping his tablet. Reyn frowned in his direction and then at the twins. "What is he doing here?"

"Well, he likes to sit with us, as always."

"Yeah, well, don't let him drink. Anyways, I am going. Is Ashley there?"

"No, she's drinking," said Lappy, walking towards them with his innocent eyes.

"Really, inside?"

"Nope, at her home. Just kidding — I've no idea."

Reyn shook her head. "You're never going to be serious. Either way, if I need help, I will call you guys. Just inform Maverick to be on standby. Where is he now?"

"He's in there, smoking up a storm. Where are you going, though? Will Jack be with you?" asked Ferrell.

Reyn considered explaining, but decided against it. She squished Lappy's puffy cheeks and then quickly hugged the twins, and was about to swivel back to her path once again.

"Wait, though. Here…" muttered Ferrell, reaching in his jacket's waist pocket, and pulling out a metal ball. "If you get caught in immediate danger where you can't inform us, this ball will sense it and beep us back here."

"Thank you, guys, so much…"

But then Lappy rushed forward and held out his holographic tablet. "I am sorry I don't have any gadgets now. But if you get bored on your way, I have a thousand games…"

"Guys, stop!" Reyn waved it away, half-laughing and half-tearful. "I love you all so much, but if I wait another moment here, I am going to lose my resolution to get out of here." And then she left, slinking the metal ball down in one of the backpack side pockets as she ran.

The spiralling staircase and the invisible ripple-fall finally brought her to the surface and into the grim, narrow, winding hall with a misshapen staircase squished tightly in an already limited passageway. She inhaled in unnerved, shallow breaths, as she made her way through the foyer, eyeing the thin wooden door of the entrance. Any moment now, she'd see the sky, a big blue expanse that most of her people only dreamt of in songs.

The light burst into the passageway as she opened the door, and burnt deep imprints in her mind. Already, the surface was bright as heavens, lit by a star itself, and it was unlike any weak artificial lighting. She squinted, feeling for the handle and shutting the door behind her. Immediately, she stumbled and came close to smashing face-first into the pavement as her feet found their way through the crooked, concrete doorsteps.

Her eyes were still struggling to adjust, causing her to totter towards the middle of the road, where she turned back to look at the house that she had come from. It was a frail figure sandwiched between two taller structures, its lopsided roof and the blue paint withering away.

Finally, she dared to look at the sky, and almost slumped helplessly to the floor when the blue, insurmountable expanse of the space struck her. The vast expanse of it was smothering for her, as if weighing down on the earth itself. Overcome by dizziness and legs which had become unresponsive under her, she kept staring, looking for an apex, or a comforting end. A car harshly honked at her, so she gawked at it confusedly, and then made to move away, only to crash against one of the parked cars on the suburban street. A couple of stringent and business-faced people walked by on the pavement, scowling at her condescendingly. They walked like soulless machines scuttling to their businesses, lacking any awareness whatsoever.

Befuddled and erratic, she pulled out her phone from the pocket of her leather jacket. Feeling no longer planned and prepared, she wasn't so confident any more of finding Alex's place. But that was where Jack told her he'd be at the end of his trip, right? Maybe so, but she didn't really know if she could navigate through the convoluted streets of New York. Maybe she could reach the main road outside the suburb and find some public transport. Yes, that seemed a better plan, or at least a stable place to start.

She took to the pavement on the opposite side of the road, and then started making her way to the main road, fully aware of the suspicious glances from the people sparsely walking by. After all, a jet-black jacket and combat leggings didn't look so civilian-friendly, and that was before accounting for her overstuffed backpack.

Either way, she made her way with quick strides, noticing how the houses were decorated with white and blue poinsettias, golden and red eye-shaped garlands festooned on the walls, the ornaments hanging on trees written with verses from the *Tome*. Many houses even had a white, satin banner doused in red ink with the phrase which highlighted the date when the parade would reach Sancta America: "The parade reaches February first, repent for the Paragon!"

She felt quite sick, honestly, as if all of this was just a mockery of Christmas.

Suddenly, as she assimilated her surroundings, it was at a corner where she walked into someone. The person gasped sharply as her forehead rammed into their trachea. She staggered back, wide-eyed and alarmed, only to see a confused Jack, rubbing his neck and with a perplexed expression.

An hour later, the train sped seamlessly while the warm, vibrant scenery of the blooming spring passed by. There were maple trees, glistening red and proud, branded in their flamboyance, and the red apple trees bursting with fruition. Her favourites were Japanese cherry blossoms with their majestic pink blanket of leaves fluttering to the floor. She smiled broadly, unable to hold her amusement as she peered through the window like a curious kitten. She had never seen this much colour — because, well… the Dark's cavern didn't have these trees, only the good old oaks and willows or whatever; just normal trees.

Her biggest amusement, though, was that this NYC, unlike the one four hundred years ago, wasn't littered with skyscrapers or taller structures. The concrete jungle had become sparse, almost halved compared to the pictures they had from history, and nature had really overtaken the rest. After all, Paragon nuked much of Asia and Africa and turned them into a forest. He really did love his nature.

But there was something she found particularly weird. "It's bizarre, it all seems so small now."

Jack, who was sitting beside her, turned towards her, understanding what she meant. "We do have the 'scrapers, but they're scarce. It's all underground now, but we have hovering cars, four rotors on them, but they aren't made to fly. They're exclusively permitted in our underground tunnel network only. You should see them; maybe I will show you. We will leave the train at the next station."

"All right!" She nodded excitedly for whatever adventure which came her way.

Jack tapped the window sill, sending out the seamless tune he always did, but didn't remember where from. He seemed happy, which was like a blossoming flower in a rigid winter.

"What's with that dumb smile on that sad mug?" Reyn teased, poking him in the waist.

He jumped back, laughing. "I don't know. I feel good, like a good start."

"Like something good is going to happen?"

"Yeah, as cliché as it sounds, but I feel like things are starting to piece together."

"That's good, you know. I am glad — I guess it has something to do with your breakthrough mystery which you haven't told me about yet."

He frowned for a moment, and then his eyes lit up with realisation. "Oh, yes, you won't believe what I found. Ernaline literally left a message for the knight in her farewell letter. Talk about love transcending all your predestined barriers."

She gaped at him incredulously. "Really? You aren't just screwing with me, right?"

"Nope, more like the knight never got to screw with her."

Reyn rolled her eyes hard enough to see her skull, but they both broke into laughter. "All right then, show me what you got."

He smirked and reached for his backpack, briefly opening the zip, and then prodded in stealthily to find the tablet, even though the whole train compartment was empty. That didn't last long, though, as the train quickly came to a halt, and before they realised, the people were filling in from the next station. He then zipped it back resignedly and they both left the station to catch an underground ride. It would only take a couple of hours to reach with it, while with the train it would have been longer. Either way, she would have to restrain her curiosity regarding what he was going to show her.

When they reached the subway-like entrance by a swift walk through the block, it was going to be her first time seeing a hovering car in real life. As they climbed down the stairs, it became darker, lit only by the daylight behind them and the dim light seeping from the platform down below. She noticed everything, every little detail, and just imbibed it like she had the previous scenarios; the cool silver railing between them, the obsidian tiles covering the tunnel wrapped around them. And when they reached the bottom, finally, a rather funny sign said:

"Underground passage for car access,

Access for underground car passage."

Her eyebrows rose in surprise as she read it, and then she giggled. Jack made a face in confusion, so she pointed at the sign. He shook his head dismissively.

"Well, that's rather tautological," she teased.

"Screw that word."

"Why?"

"It just sounds so pretentious."

"Ugh," she grunted, "all right then, I will simmer it down for you, captain I-am-always-right."

They bickered right there on the edge of the platform, waiting for a car to stop by. The platform was, in fact, no wider than a regular pavement, stretching to ten metres only on either side. And in front were two roads meant for the cars to travel. It was, in all honesty, like an underground roadway. A few moments went by, and a brown car gently hovered to a standstill in front of them, gleaming under the dim, pale lighting of the tunnel. At the bottom, instead of four wheels, it had four rotors about a metre in diameter attached to it, all encased and thoroughly secured to avoid any casualties. The car itself was sleek and aerodynamic like a sports car, but slightly longer in length, like a limo. The whirring of the rotors was surprisingly quiet, and when they went to sit in, after Jack had negotiated the place they wanted to be, she stepped over a small step built at the door, meant to leverage a passenger, as the cars were kept levitating a foot off the ground.

The ride was unexpectedly smooth, too smooth, in fact. No bumping, no jittering over fissures on the road; just a smooth, aerial ride. She clutched the seat, feeling slightly nauseous. Is this how it feels to be in an airplane? Maybc it did; but either way, she quickly got used to the seamless movements and found herself losing to sleep as the gentle sways of it turning corners and going round the crossways felt endearing, like a baby's cradle.

It was about an hour later that, quite reluctant and groggily, she had to follow him to a hotel lobby as the car dropped them off at one of the underground stops nearby. It seemed to be quite a commodious one, nothing short of expensive, she guessed. Before she could ask, and before they approached the counter, he hesitantly stopped for a moment and pursed his lips.

"I think you should stay at this hotel while I go meet him," he muttered hesitantly.

"Yup, I really think you should."

"I mean I know, but his family will be there; it might get awkward. I don't want to make it uncomfortable after everything that happened, you know?"

"I understand," said Reyn, patting his arm. She then glanced around the luxurious hotel surroundings. "Are you paying for it?"

"Yeah, sure. Just stay here for a bit until I get back."

"But it's so unnecessary and expensive."

'Yup; no problem, though. Consider me the Batman of your organisation."

She chuckled, shaking her head. "Oh my God, except you wish you were as cool as him."

"Yeah, right; it's not like your stupid little cavern is anywhere near as interesting as Gotham, either."

"What did you just say?"

"That's right; seems like this little cave person beside me also has some hearing difficulties."

"You're just ridiculous."

He smirked, pointed her towards the room, and then left.

Shades of mauve

Jack stood across the street in front of Alex's house. The shore was not far away to their right, as the water sloshed against the rocky beach and broke into a foamy spray. The house stood proud at the ground level of the building, with a column of similar large houses stacked above it. In front, the balcony and the porch alike were covered with vines. It was wide and roomy in structure, and as he approached the porch, with the walls covered in vines creeping around the main entrance, he noticed that the windows were open, as the curtains blew with a hollow whirl. He knocked on the red door, waiting patiently for someone to respond.

He had been here once or twice, on their summer trips, usually; he knew his mother and the father, and his three siblings; all handsome and comely, like him. His mother especially, with a short, blonde cut sweeping across the face, and a sparkling white smile, really resembled Alex. She'd be the most welcoming to Jack, always with that coquettish smile. Jack smiled to himself, remembering Alex's embarrassment whenever his mother would swivel their way down the stairs and tried to speak with them.

Jack knocked once again, only realising that the hall showing through the glass etchings on the door was completely empty.

"Alex…! Alex…! Mrs Dylan!" he called out, but no one replied. He then noticed that there were no cars parked in front of the house. Perhaps they were all gone, maybe? He pulled out the temporary phone which Reyn had given to him, and checked the message he had sent.

Hey there, I am back! Gonna come see you…

Okay, I realise I disappeared like that… The place is nice, but I lost my phone.

There was no reply to these messages. He walked up to one of the windows beside the main door, and through the blowing curtain he saw once again that the house was empty. The lights were off, and the only light coming through were from the windows and the opposite side of the hall. The red curtains solemnly blew in the warm air, and the beam of sunlight fell on the two red sofas and the table in the middle of the hall. He found it strange that they had left the windows open like this.

He knocked once again, and then impulsively decided to check the handle. It actually unlocked, and the door opened with a click. He scowled as he entered. Something didn't feel right. Maybe someone was at home, just unable to hear him. It wasn't a big deal; he was always welcomed to just walk in like a member of family.

He entered the home and walked through the hall. To his left was the main staircase leading up. On the small round table between the sofas was a book with the cover stitched with red cloth. It was the *Tome of Sanctum*, he realised. It seemed so strange for him to see it now.

The hall was modestly furnished, with bookshelves stacked up on either side. He went for the staircase and climbed up, going for Alex's room. The door was closed, with just the light spilling from the crack on the floor. He is here then, he thought, and knocked on the door.

"Alex? Please open the door. I am sorry if it felt like I had ignored you for so long..."

"Alex? Really, how bad can I be? Okay, all right, no excuses. I messed up for being a jerk."

He knocked twice again, all the while thinking, all right, please be here, please be here. I won't be able to come back once I leave... He fretted for a moment and then went for thc handlc, breathing in, and then opened the door...

His friend was hanging with the rope tied to the ceiling, the eyes lifeless and face swollen purple. The only thing left was a piece of paper on the floor. '25/01/2500', it said. It was the date for the Parade reaching London, some time the next day. Whoever did this, wanted him to be there.

Young and the bold!

It was a lazy afternoon, except for the tension pervading the living room. Lappy was intent on cracking a code which was stubbornly protected from its source. Everyone else, though, was worried and curious, waiting for some sort of response from Reyn. They tried killing time their own way. Ferrell was perched on the armrest of the same couch where Lappy was laying, and he was facing Ashley, who sat similarly on the armrest of the couch adjacent to it. They played a game of chess on a small circular table placed between them.

Lappy sighed, frustrated, unable to crack the code. He rubbed his sore neck, and then peered around the room. Both Ferrell and Ashley couldn't possibly have looked more unenthusiastic about the game, while Kiara sat on a creaking chair, watching their game and drowning herself in wine. Maverick, as usual, was reading something too hefty for Lappy's taste.

"What do you think could've happened to them so far?" he asked, a question which they all had been avoiding so far.

"We have no idea, but she's supposed to send us a message if anything happens," replied Ferrell, moving his queen across the board.

"Can we all do something, please?" said Maverick, placing down the controller and stretching.

"Like running?" Ashley teased.

"Nope," Maverick said, walking towards them and pouring himself a glass from Kiara's wine. He took a sip before continuing, "Can we at least know where the damn old man is and why he's cooped us up here? If he's figured it out this quickly, then we're all done for."

However, they didn't have to ponder much about that, as soon Van Vuren came in, opening the door with a considerable force for someone as composed as him.

"Do you know what you have all done?"

No one dared say anything, except for Maverick. "No, only if you'd let us know more, they wouldn't have recklessly left."

Van Vuren sighed in a way which showed the collective burden he must have had over the past two centuries. Lappy had never seen him so tangibly stressed. Whatever the consequence of hiding the secret was he feared, seemed to have bigger stakes than they knew of.

"I've already found out that Reyn's escaped. You three…" He gazed in the direction of the twins and

Lappy. Lappy gulped, while the twins looked at the floor.

"Other elders of the city and I had hidden this from you for the sole reason that you would be too young to shoulder this responsibility. For the longest time it worked, but in light of recent events, I will clearly have to tell you. From today, you will have to realise the weight of your responsibilities." He paused, looking around the living room. They were all ears. "Have you ever wondered how our cave has remained hidden from the Sanctum? Have you wondered what makes us untraceable? Well, it is this seal. A Seal of the Eight. It makes an aura which hid entire towns from being found by the Sanctum during the war days. For us, it also connects this cave to the house on the surface, through the portal of our aura. This makes us virtually invisible and untraceable should we choose to remain hidden. To create this seal, you need eight people, each with a different state of mind. As I've told you all, power is a state of mind. So, throughout each generation, we had people vouching to be part of the seal. As we rescued Maverick last year, you children became one of the most promising groups in this generation. So I did that, and made you all into part of the seal."

"Uh, Van?" interrupted Zachary suddenly, who had just woken up. "I don't think any of us know about the ritual; so how did it happen?"

"I am the mind of this place, therefore whosoever dons the mantle of mind can choose the rest of the people required for the seal through the power which flows through this cave. Just so you know, your life-force is tied to this place now. If you leave — or, in a worse case, die — the seal weakens. So now you know what you've done: you've let Reyn run away without any supervision. As the second strongest power user in your group, her lack of presence is already weakening the aura protecting us."

Nobody had much response to that, not even Maverick, who seethed silently in the corner, squishing the controller in his hand absentmindedly. Van Vuren sighed and readjusted his sleeves before leaving, but not without one last bombshell, "I am placing you all under house arrest until we find Reyn, and I hope you realise the weight of the responsibilities which you now carry."

Everyone just stared at each other incredulously, before Ferrell went and peered through the hall window, which looked over the city. There were multiple men wearing the green, skin-tight military outfit of the Dark, complete with their blue vests. He gawked at the roof, and, sure enough, it was also already patrolled by a soldier, too. Ferrell scratched his head, dumbfounded, which was until one of the guards, readily equipped with a helmet and protective goggles, decided to look at the window. He grinned awkwardly, and spoke in a thick, country accent. "Hey there, brats, anything special? Big fan, by the way."

Maverick decided to butt in. "Yeah, could you please get us some tacos, man. I am hungry…"

"Stop it, Maverick," Ashley told him, with an icy glare.

"Ah, God dammit then, what now? Anyone want coffee? All I wanted for our misfortunate group was the means of sustenance, which Ashley has so kindly ruined."

The room started reverberating with collective groans, inaudible at first but becoming so guttural that he had to stop. "Well, then. I don't know what to do."

"Can't you blow them off with your power?" asked Lappy, mimicking the movement.

"That would be strictly stupid of me to try."

There wasn't much else to do than sitting it out, so everyone shrugged it off and resumed their activities. Kiara, for one, put the bottle down and pulled out a book to read. Zachary almost instantaneously dozed off, while Maverick, Ferrell and Ashley found Jenga pieces in one of the empty bookshelf compartments and started stacking it up. Lappy, too, resigning to the twist of fate, was almost subjugated to waiting until they were released, and started tinkering with his device yet again, only that it burst to life from an emergency line, startling the soul out of him.

Once the image settled from the incoming static, it was Reyn, frantic and puffing.

"Lappy!" she cried, and the entire room rushed and ensnared Lappy to see the screen.

"What, where are you, Reyn?" asked Ashley, retaining her calmness in this moment of exigency.

"Well listen, guys; remember that friend of Jack? He has been murdered. We are heading for London tomorrow, because that's where the date pointed to near the crime scene. Tomorrow, in London, when the parade will reach there. Listen..."

The screen went to static once again, and while everyone tried to say something, to make some sense of the situation, the screen went blank. For a moment, everyone remained silent, and then started speaking simultaneously. Lappy spoke of reporting it to Van, which Ashley agreed with. Zach and Ferrell spoke of getting weapons and leaving, and Kiara agreed with them. Maverick alone stood silent, pursing his lips and scowling.

Suddenly, he spoke. "Guys, I know what to do. Fred. Fred will get us out of here." That might have been true. Freddy, a bald, jagged-toothed, older man from the region of Scythe was practically inseparable from Maverick. Despite his age, Maverick's infatuation of Scythian culture, being Grim's birthplace and all, drew him to the man. Lappy always thought of Maverick being Fred's sidekick, kind of in a weird way.

"Well, do you think he's gonna be able to deal with the security outside? And even then, we can't all leave… Remember what Van said about the seal?" Ashley asked concernedly about their plan.

"Let's see what he can suggest…" He then went to the intercom on the wall across the room, which connected all the houses and businesses in the entire city for ease of communication. He took the white receiver and then dialled the number, the digits softly glowing green with his touch.

"Hey? Hey there, Fred?" he inquired as the call connected. "I don't know if you know, but the old man has trapped us in the house; he's trying to find Reyn and stuff…"

"Yeah, yeah, I know it very well. Ha, ha, bad luck for you kiddies, I guess."

"No, you cheeky bastard, get us out of here, if you can. And hey, do you know about the seal…?"

"Yes, I know. It's not really true. Unless you all die outside, it will be intact. I'll guide you, don't worry."

"All right. The house is protected by some soldiers, by the way."

"I'll take those brats out." And the intercom disconnected.

Maverick looked at the group for ascent, and they nodded without a visible rebuke. Soon enough, with the sound of four quick snaps, they saw two soldiers from the roof fall off, sprawling unconsciously near their mates on the ground. The group rushed concernedly to the window, to see if they weren't legitimately hurt, even though the shots were easily distinguishable tranquillisers.

From the steep hill curving in the window view, Freddie appeared walking up. He disabled the lock and then stepped in.

"All right, kids, what's the deal?"

"Uh, Fred," said Maverick, "we just got a call from Reyn; she's already left for London…"

"Oh, bloody hell. Van Vuren's gonna have a hell of a time tracking her, then."

"But that's not it; they're going to the parade, and anything can happen…"

"Hah. They would get flattened."

"I know, you bald-ass, which is why I ask: what should we do now?"

"Hmph…" Fred rubbed his chin. "We will go to the parade, all of us. As one group, we can save them."

Ashley seemed sceptical at the sound of that. "Uh, guys, is it really a good idea to go all together, in the riskiest part, with what Van said and everything…?"

Lappy kind of agreed with her, but could tell from the looks on the faces of the boys, and especially Maverick, that they didn't like her doubts.

"Yeah, we'll be fine if Fred's along with us. And what's up with you, always trying to be the good girl? It gets annoying. Go cry to your parents if you're scared," Maverick mocked Ashley in her own tone of speaking.

Her concerned and innocent expression turned into a scowl. They both frowned at each other, growling, acting like pissed-off cats. Lappy squealed a little, always excited to ship them in these situations. They both glanced at him, and broke the stare-down as they blushed.

"Well, if ya kids are done bickering, I've got a plan. Listen, if you all leave, Vanesse and Van would be the only ones left. Van is part of the seal, besides you seven, which means that he will have to be trapped until we return," said Fred, looking at each of them.

"He's gonna be beyond furious when we come back..." Ashley told him matter-of-factly, not completely on board with the insanity.

"Nah, you just have to prove yourself worthy and he'll suck it up."

And that was that, then. They didn't spare much time, packing up their weapons and provisions. They considered changing clothes, since a bunch of them would look unusual clad in their usual attire; the twins wore their usual white T-shirt and sleeveless camo jackets, complete with camo trousers and ranger boots. Ashley, with her petite frame, always wore a white T-shirt too large for her, a black unbuttoned waistcoat, black jeans and fingerless gloves. Maverick, like Lappy, didn't have to change, wearing an overcoat, with a casual shirt and trousers, while Lappy remained in his usual blue windbreaker a bit too large for him, his elastic jeans, and dirty white joggers. Kiara remained unchanged, too, with her black tank top and jeans.

After a couple of minutes, the twins switched their camo trousers and boots for casual denims and sneakers. Ashley just took off her waistcoat and the gloves and switched the T-shirt out for a loose orange one.

After that, they hoisted their bags up, trickled down the hill, and traversed their way from outside the city wall, heading for the main gate. Lappy felt adrenaline coursing through his veins, since it was his first time leaving for the outside. He saw the intricate symbol of a glowing sun carefully chiselled and embossed on the gate. They stepped outside, and were picked up by a force like ripples of water. Lappy had never felt more euphoric than the moment he was submerged into it.

Change of plans

It was seven in the evening, and the sky was tinged an obscure shade of twilight blue. Twilight was always indistinguishable to Maverick from the shades of dawn. For all he worried, he wished that it was the morning instead, where they'd be in the Sancta Europa already, waiting for the evening and finding Reyn and Jack again. Instead, right now, they were stuck walking down the streets of Storm, New York, previously known as Queens in the old times. He dug out his Common Registry device once again, glimpsing his picture with a fake tracking chip and the number written below. It would help them bypass through the airport, though he remembered the older device that he used to have before he was rescued by the Dark.

Truth be told, he loved the Dark. He loved their culture and history. He loved the revolutionary stories dating back from olden empires — their architecture which was preserved through copied landscapes. However, he was thrilled to be on the surface once again, imagining that one day he'd be able to participate in a war which would finally defeat the Sanctum.

However, there were smaller and more exigent problems at hand, one being the six Sanctum guards walking down the street. They had their black batons of disintegration holstered at their hips, while they were covered in a full, white, skeleton armour. The glass on their visors was dark and lifeless. He heard Freddie curse under his breath, as they went through the lone, narrow street with the walk-up apartments on either side.

Before, it had seemed safe enough for a group of eight people to walk through, which didn't seem to be the case any more. Maverick kept his composure, and glanced at his mates. Zachary and Ferrell, being experienced, remained nonchalant, while Lappy seemed to be fidgeting with his phone. Kiara smoked through, uncaring, taking drags and puffing it up in the air. It was only Ashley who quizzically met his gaze, her hazel green eyes glowing anxiously under the street lights.

He nodded to her reassuringly. As they almost brushed past the guards, the guards decided to stop dead in their tracks, staring at them through their black, impenetrable visors.

Next thing Maverick knew was back-pedalling from two guards at once, desperately trying to avoid their swinging batons, a glance from which could disintegrate his flesh like acid. He held out both his hands, concentrated, and felt his hands submerge into ripples like water. And then he blew those ripples out, sending a guard stumbling and the other sprawling. He only had a moment to glance towards the twins swinging their backpacks, trying to distance the guards, and then his own assailants were back at him, swinging the batons. Their gauntlets hummed each time with a movement from the electric current flowing inside. He held up his hands once again, except a guard almost got close enough to land the baton on it, startling Maverick and causing him to jump back; and then the other guard was in, glazing the baton through the skin of his right wrist, causing him to back off completely. He brought his hands down, felt the ripples, and, like shooting up on a trampoline, he was off his feet and landed a few metres back. Beside him, he saw Ashley stumbling and falling on her ass, as she barely held the lightning-discharge rifle, while a guard closed in on her. Maverick raised his hands out again and with a burst of rage, two of the three guards went flying, hitting a truck and becoming unresponsive. The third guard only caught a glancing blow, edging onto Ashley, but this time she let loose a blinding zap of lightning and he dropped down, his white armour charred black in places.

Both Maverick and Ashley glanced at each other and nodded. To their right, Kiara performed an illusion on the guards, making them scream and flail from their phantom terror, while Zachary and Ferrell finally took them out. To their left, with Freddie and a guard going hand to hand and blow for blow, the guard managed to land a solid punch with a zap of his electric gauntlet to Fred's gut. Fred keeled over, breathless from the punch. But before the guard could even flinch, Fred's dagger had stabbed through the vulnerable black fabric in the exoskeleton suit exposing his gut. The guard stiffened and fell unconscious.

Meanwhile, from somewhere, Lappy ran screeching between all of them as a seventh guard came chasing after him while flailing his baton, but was put down with multiple zaps of lightning.

"Holy cow, Lappy, where did you come from?" wondered Maverick aloud.

"More like, where did *he* come from?" Ashley pointed to the seventh guard, which now laid at the ground.

"Actually, where did they all come from?" yelled both the twins in unison; and, sure enough, there was a military jeep-tank hybrid rolling around the corner.

They all ran, and in the midst of their confusion as to which alley to scramble into, a bolt of lightning, so bright that it could have blinded the viewer, zapped past them and then razed the wall at the end of the street. The sound of the discharge left Maverick's ears ringing, and the flash rendered him almost blind. They shot to their left, taking a narrow alleyway. It was too narrow for the vehicle to go through, and they quickly dissipated within the network of an overpopulated neighbourhood. It wasn't over, though, as a few soldiers from the jeep hopped off and caught on their tail, sending bolts of lightning behind them. To counter this, Zachary and Ferrell turned around and shot their own.

There were about four soldiers on their tail, and the best would be to ambush them, which they just did. They quickly turned a corner and broke through a rusted door beside a massive dumpster. They chose wave blasters this time, to silently fry their brains in this close-ranged alley, and then the twins swung their way up the stairs and crouched at the first storey. Maverick and Kiara were beside the dumpster. Ashley and Lappy remained hidden behind the rusted door, prepared with the wave blasters aimed at the entrance.

Just as the soldiers were about to pass through, the twins from the stairs, and Maverick and Kiara beside the dumpster, sprang out and pulled their triggers, and within moments the soldiers fell lifelessly to the floor, incapacitated by the microwaves.

Fred immediately rushed out, ushering Ashley and Lappy with him, and aggressively signalled for the twins to climb down. When they were all assembled, he gushed in an urgent tone, "Right, kids, I've no idea why, but I didn't expect to be caught like this. I will try and dispose of these bodies and return to the city. The airport is close by; you should rush there and make sure to act normal and not like a retard. If any of these roaches try to follow up our trail, I will make sure to kill 'em."

As they nodded and turned their backs to him and began walking, Maverick tried to stay and mouth his protest, but Fred was having none of it. Maverick sighed and walked along with the group, except what happened during the next few seconds could possibly change everything.

There was a blinding flare, like a flash powder attack, rendering him momentarily visionless. As the white noise gave way to the shape of the surroundings, he saw Fred heavily cursing and pummelling the head of one of the soldier's into the floor. The soldier had feigned being dead, Maverick quickly realised. On the floor next to them was Kiara, stabbed through with a gaping hole, and he frantically dropped down, trying to bind the wound through his power. She whimpered even louder as he desperately tried to hold her. His mind went back to all the people he had possibly killed, except this time he was the one suffering the consequences of killing.

Fred spoke with someone on his phone, to which he paid no heed. Ashely was with them instantly, placing her hand on the wound. As a powerful healer, she could fix this soon. The twins and Lappy stood completely still, shocked from what had just transpired.

As he spoke words of reassurance to Kiara, he heard the distant murmur of Fred addressing the phone:

“Vanesse… listen…” But he was told off and the call was cut.

Fred turned to Maverick, sighing. “You kids go, I will get her back.”

“I will need some time to heal her wound!” cried Ashley, shaking from the ordeal.

Kiara raised her hand and placed it over Ashley’s. “Go… it already feels better. I will go back.” Ashley protested, but Kiara very slightly shook her head. “No.”

Fred quickly rushed to them, and with their assistance, bound Kiara’s waist with the yellow satin cloth. It was infused with a healer’s power and would maintain her until they reached the Dark.

Fred nodded to them all. “It will be all right, kids, and we’re gettin’ back-up. I will deal with the consequences.”

They had no choice but to glance at Fred and Kiara one last time as they rushed through the alley as quickly as possible.

Morning before the parade

A chill Monday it was, under the overcast sky of London. As Jack gazed through the misty glass, looking over an empty park glistening with the night's drizzle, he contemplated the contrast of his own inner state versus the green, peaceful serenity. It was the twenty-sixth today, and at approximately five in the evening, they would be heading towards the parade. Truth be told, he felt nothing. Not numb, not even nervous, nor even sad from… from what? He'd buried everything which happened yesterday. But burying pain is never effective; it mends anguish only for so long before the crudely stitched-away pain festers from the inside.

He glimpsed at his watch: eight in the morning. Reyn must have been sleeping, or not. They had argued, with him unfairly raging on her. The image of the Sanctum in his head had burned itself with hatred. The text written by Ernaline flashed in his mind yet again: "Griffith, my baby boy…" How could the world be so cruel to individuals like them? Something still didn't make sense of the whole thing, but he had buried his logic as well.

Either way, he exhaled through his nose disdainfully and walked off, heading towards the park beneath the hotel building. It was definitely chill, his favourite weather. He loved the overcast skies and scornful bleakness, something about it which he always found endearing.

Striding through the walkway, the aromatic smell of the grass, like warmth and the slight bitterness, combined with the cold breeze sneaking through his overcoat, felt really therapeutic. From a slight distance, he saw pigeons flocking near a bench hidden by overgrown bushes on its sides. When he almost walked past it, he saw a very similar face, to his surprise.

"Mr Beck?" he spluttered.

Mr Beck was jolted from his little trance. "Good lord, it is you, Jack."

"Yes, I guess…"

"Well, hello there." He gestured towards the empty place on the large bench. "You can have a seat."

"Um, thank you, but I am fine. I was meant to just walk by."

"Oh, it does not have to be this way. Yes, I may not be your boss any more, but please accept this nice gesture for me. I understand the weight of circumstances which you must have come to pass."

Jack sighed, and walked towards the bench, careful to not scare the flock of pigeons, and slumped down on the bench, obviously not ready for questions. But Mr Beck didn't evoke any; instead, he said, "I can only imagine what you must've seen when you disappeared. Maybe it entailed questioning the very nature of what you believed was true..." Mr Beck paused for a moment, but Jack just remained silent. "Just like you, I was always curious about the objectiveness of this world... of the rationality of beliefs, and what justifies anything which we do consider to be justified. What is it which decides the nature of an action to be just? Morality? Perhaps. But we all seek to justify the nature of one thing or another." He paused, smiling as if remembering something. "Allen had to die for something which he did not do, but it happened all the same. It is like our job as cogs in a wheel, huh? He died a middleman, a victim of the turnings of fate. I am sure you must, too, have felt the impact of the undulations of fate on your path?"

Jack just nodded; that was exactly how it was. But he wondered what Mr Beck would feel had he gone through the experience himself.

"So... what brings you here to London?" Beck asked, with an understanding look.

Jack remained idly staring at the grass for a moment or two, pondering if he had the energy to gather and speak his thoughts. Finally, he heaved a breath, mustering an answer. “Let’s just say, whichever place I was in, I had to leave after some discoveries… If I could, I would wish for none of this to have ever happened.”

“Oh, my…” said Beck. “But you can’t tell me, can you?”

“No…”

“Ah, I understand. Such is life. I will trouble you no more…” And he did as he promised, going silent, back to finding his way into the large, white bag of sunflower seeds and then throwing them to the pigeons.

Eventually, despite everything, Jack found himself asking, “Mr Beck, have you ever found yourself questioning your purpose… or your worth in this world? The worth of this world?”

“Well, of course. When you start young, you find yourself to be passionate and visionary. As you approach adulthood, you find yourself wiser and perhaps more cynical. But as you reach even farther in life, you see even beyond what most people don’t see…”

“What do you see, then?”

“I don’t know.” He chuckled heartily. “Ah, I apologise, but pardon me, the pigeons must be fed. They peck their heads like we bow, seeking sustenance as we seek salvation.” He chuckled yet again, but Jack remained hunched as miserably as ever before.

"Ah, but I understand you. Here, have some seeds..." said Beck, placing the bag of seeds between them. "Let your pain seethe away in an act of goodwill. If you hold the pain back, eventually it will last enough for the world to see it. And that's never good."

Jack sighed, taking the seeds involuntarily. "You know, Mr Beck, maybe you do actually make sense. Back at the office, the legend was wrong, that you just blabbered mindlessly..."

"Why'd you assume in the first place that the legends were untrue? You seriously hurt my pride that way. I am quite a jester myself."

Even Jack had to smile at that. Beck went silent once again, letting Jack have his space. Jack felt slightly eased now, breathing in the fresh air, while finding the activity also quite therapeutic.

"Jack, have you ever heard the tale of a boy who turned god?" Beck asked after a while.

"Not really... but go ahead."

"All right then. The story was about a boy like you a long time ago. He had three friends, and two of them would frivolously indulge in idle talk, spending time in matters he considered worthless. He would worry about the world, yet he was looked down upon as an odd individual for his concerns. Soon enough, he found himself detached completely, and out of the circle, growing bitter with apathy, until the very day that he decided to reunite with his three friends on the bridge over the river. That night, he was glad to see his third friend, the friend who always talked well of him, no matter what the circumstances were. After a while, sitting there and having a few laughs, once again, he realised that he was being prised apart from the matters which were actually important. As the night went on, watching them jest, watching them bicker, he once again tried bringing up matters of importance; instead, he became the topic of the joke. He wished then that if he were a god, he'd set the universe right. And just like that, he felt his vision become omniscient. He had gained the intrinsic knowledge of all; he could create, vanish, and warp as he willed, breathing the very laws of the universe itself, rendering his intelligence beyond mortal understanding. Soon enough, he thought, he was a God beyond eternity. He did not require the mortals. And so, with a blink, humanity vanished. For moments perhaps, it seemed to be fine to be the only one to exist, but then the silence pierced him harder than any mean judgment. It was him, and no one else. It started boggling him to realise how existence as a concept ceased to exist when it was only him that could recognise it. The more he thought, the more he realised, and finally he asked himself the foreboding question: 'If nothing existed to acknowledge his existence, then did he, in fact, exist at all?'

"Such questions bothered him, until he was far away; but far away from what? Everything around him was his creation, but also an empty echo chamber for eternity. It was when he came upon a small shore beside a cliff, where he settled from the flight, and then walked by remembering his past. The water was clearest there. The sand was the softest, and the small rock structures which had formed at the shore where the water splashed, looked too beautiful to be natural, as if they were man-made. It was then with a smile, comparing the now lifeless shore with the earnest scenery from the past, that he realised that his creation was too beautiful to go unnoticed. And so, he birthed a civilisation and life yet again. As eternity passed, he busied himself watching the evolution of his own creatures, of them finding their way. When intelligence flourished once again, and started struggling against the calamities of the world, he'd appear as a friend, following the same concept of friendship that had made him fearful and bound in the past. As time passed, his little indulgences somehow became a myth; tales that god, indeed, had many faces that he'd use to befriend his loving creations. But, by then he was intangible and lost, somewhere deep in the universe, tangled yet again in doubts, questioning why any of it mattered in the face of eternity. And so he discovered the only answer to his conflict: that he himself didn't understand the truth which he had forced his people to believe."

Beck stopped for a while before he spoke again, but this time in a graver tone, his voice as deep and serene as ever. "It is hard to lose, Jack. And the loss never goes away. But in order for greater things to happen, sacrifices must be made…"

Once he had finished, the surroundings felt eerily silent to Jack. He didn't know if he wanted to be a part of the conversation any more. "All right then, Mr Beck, I will see you again…" he said, and got up and left. All he had left now was to wait for the evening. It was time for him to move forward. To take what was his. No matter what it would take to fix this world now, he was willing to pay.

The parade begins

The air was palpably humid, plastering her hair on her cheeks and neck. The sun slyly broke through the clouds and pierced her eyes while she was still recovering from a deep sleep. She squinted, struggling against the sunlight, while having to sweep her hair behind her ears. Reyn had always been a deep sleeper, like a pup after a full day of walking, and was equally as snappy and irritable when awakened. Jack had dragged her out at eleven in the morning, while he himself looked even more miserable and sleep-deprived.

"So, where are we going again?"

"Gonna look around London," Jack responded staidly.

And that was that; but something she noticed quite prominently was that the whole city was exuberant and on the streets. Children, adults and everyone alike were wearing white sashes and Sanctum flag pins. The parks were bustling with people, especially with shenanigans of the Sanctum religion; masks like the flag's bleeding eye, of mock armours like the knights and the white and blue lordly tunics of the royal families. Children ran past her toting props of the knight's weaponry or repeating scenes from the Sanctum *Tome* with events that were supposed to depict World War Three.

While turning into one street in particular, she saw a large screen etched on a building, with an arrow pointing towards the direction of where Big Ben would be, towards Westminster London, if she guessed it right, though there was no Big Ben any more or Westminster palace. Along with the pre-war history were gone the prominent British landmarks as well. The Westminster area in particular was just called the High Tower area.

Upon that sign was written the preliminary cautions, timings and ticket reservation information for various events, some of which she read:

"Repent for the Paragon! Head towards parade at 5pm, High Tower area..."

"Please do not forget your CR devices. Stay alert about your children if you take them from the boarding, and please refrain from hassling authorities, as the crowds will be in the hundreds of thousands."

And in another column:

"These are 95% discounted tickets for viewing the palaces today!"

"Get your tickets today for spectator seats with the holy families! — Follow the link and the colour code for each family..."

She ignored this and just read the names of the families instead: Rosendale, Beckinsale, Ashdale, Trysdale, Vale, Sorrowsgale, Raellslov.

"Hmph!" she wondered aloud. "It's ridiculous how these rhyme; well, most of them."

"Yes. These are the royal families, called the Dale or the Vale families. From the verses in the tomb, and the Sanctum's point of view, these are families made of the people who originally helped Paragon beat the heretic population and save this planet. As such, they were ordained as the houses of the Sanctum. The Raellslovs, just like the name, are the odd ones and the scariest — even the people seem to fear them and take their name cautiously. They were formed from the band of bombers who nuked out most of the mid-forest region area, and would work in extreme, radioactive environments to clean up the mess. From what I read from the Dark's literature, this group is the Sanctum's nest of sleeper agents and the carrier of their biological warfare. That's what the Raellslov prison in the world is named after, as well."

"Wow!" Reyn whispered. "And I forgot much of them, even though I learned it in school."

"Eh, it happens, though all of these families have an interesting history, kind of like part of yours."

"You know there's a conspiracy in some of our people that Dark never lost the fourth battle with pride but retreated and left Grim for capture, saying that he's still in Raellslov..."

"Ah yes, I remember. Maverick used to be a part of those people."

During their back and forth, Reyn completely felt it. Felt how his responses were deeply plastic; he either looked down or averted his gaze to avoid any contact, spoke in a monotonous voice of genuine disinterest. He was burying what had happened yesterday, but she wasn't going to speak of it any more. She didn't even know how to console him, given his situation.

And the last time she tried, it became the cause of the argument before she went to sleep in the hotel. But either way, they continued walking. She noticed some children running from the school, which was just a structure of a large grey block. They had grins on their faces spreading ear to ear, while their uniforms were pinned with the bleeding eye badges meant for the pupils. They were welcomed by the families and crushed with hugs and kisses. What a miserable system, she thought; the idea of administering toddlers into boarding until they were eighteen, and only released during vacations, was honestly nauseating for her to digest.

"And they look perfectly fine with it..." she muttered to herself.

"Well, it's a part of their belief system; they do not find it abnormal," said Jack.

"But it is repulsive, yes?"

"Yes, you can say that."

"Do you ever miss it?"

Jack paused there for a moment, pursing his lips. "I was a lost child. Had no home, so... But sure, it was all right. Come on, then," he beckoned her, pointing towards a street. "I told you of the underground world, didn't I? Let's show you what it's like."

They then went through the street and entered an area with shopping complexes, which were swarming with people like locusts in the summer. Everything, indeed, was ninety-five percent off, and although that was surprising for her, with all the clothes she could get, it still wasn't the astonishing part. It was something she only realised when they stepped through the entrance of a mall, and Jack asked her to close her eyes, followed by a rather prolonged walk and a trip down an elevator.

Upon opening her eyes, she found herself nearly fifty floors beneath a colossal mall with its floors shaped like a triangle. It went up as far as she could see, with some floors made of tiles while others were mostly of glass, allowing her to look through. In the air at the top-most floor were three glass-enclosed walkways connecting in the middle, allowing people to cross to the sides.

Some levels completely baffled her, like the multiple floors which were turned into a huge forested habitat closely mimicking a rain forest, complete with little creeks, waterfalls and hills. There was a virtual gaming floor, the biggest that she'd ever seen. It would turn into a simulation of whichever game the users played. And finally, below her, something that she almost tripped by seeing, was an aquarium covered by the glass floor she stood upon.

"Jesus…" she whispered.

"Careful," murmured Jack.

"No wonder I thought buildings were so short on the surface and everything was so much greener," Reyn whispered yet again, still looking up at the prodigious structure.

"That's how it is," said Jack, smiling. "Paragon loves nature, so he made us all scuffle under the surface. But this is far from it. We've become a little bit more creative. There are restaurants on the ocean floor. We even grow modified crops down there. Hell, the biggest theme park in the world is under the ocean, the size of your city; it's located at Sancta Asia."

"You'd think someone like him would be the last to care about nature, yet it is true," said Reyn, tilting her head.

The evening was approaching soon as they wandered through London, finally deciding to go to the High Tower area. Some time in the afternoon, Jack had leaned against a lamp-post while they walked and began sobbing. She had nothing to offer but words of comfort and some water, but now he seemed to be at least slightly relieved. Reyn had checked her phone, only to find that it was out of charge, which would make her untraceable and unable to contact the group back in Dark. Unknown to Jack, she had contacted the group yesterday. She sighed; at least they had made it this far, although she had no idea what to expect at the parade or what Jack wanted to do there. But she was going to stay wary; she knew that he was on impulses now, waiting to explode.

As they got nearer, the breeze became chiller and the sky became clear, with only wisps of clouds. People were now walking towards the area, huddling into masses. Cars were banned for the day, as they would only help clutter the streets. They found one of the best spots, right near the High Tower, which was just a tall, dark blue obelisk, almost appearing black in places where the sunlight didn't fall. The palace, too, was a dark bluish block with almost no hint of its pre-war appearance. Its walls were just smooth, tiled and extremely polished, and the shade of the deep blue of the night sky. There were multiple storeys with a row of large, arched windows with interesting geometric tracery, which seemed like a pattern of circles-within-triangles-within-a-circle. This type of architecture was new to her: very simple yet intricate, but far from a Romanesque or gothic style in complexity.

It took a great deal of effort to tear her gaze away from the alluring darkness of the palace and look around. The white military jeep-tanks were now deployed, blocking the streets to stop people from spilling over to the main road leading from the bridge over the River Thames, while the guards and soldiers restricted people on the pavements. She was being pushed around mercilessly as people tried to shove and wangle their way in, and she caught Jack's hand instinctively as he was almost pulled away with the undulating mass. It was now five minutes till the parade was to begin, and before she knew it, gritting her teeth and struggling to maintain her foothold, the crowd became staid, and the parade began.

First, from the far end of the bridge, she felt the floor shake with the booming of base drums, followed by a chorus of a thousand sticks hitting the drums, and then with the bagpipes shrilling, a marching orchestra began. With a ceremonious tune she didn't know, a few thousand men marched forward in perfect synchronisation. They were dressed in red shirts with large, white epaulettes on either shoulder embroidered with golden thread. The two pockets on their shirts were lined with hefty, glimmering, gold and silver honorary badges which they'd received for religious services. Their trousers were white, strapped with thick, brown belts with a big golden buckle at their waist, and they wore deep red, high ankle shoes. They eventually crossed the bridge getting nearer, and as they did, the people started clapping along and singing with the melody:

"The Lord has arrived through,

Leading with his lantern,

Paragon we shall repent, seeking guidance from the *Tome*,

The colour has been brought to our land, to our land,

To our land, is the colour of the green brought…?"

With the overwhelming number of people, who had to join in, it was surprisingly light-hearted and catchy, but she felt uncomfortable having the words roll off her tongue. She glanced at Jack: his lips barely seemed to be moving while he lightly bobbed his head up and down, with his hair flowing with each movement.

After a few more choruses, the drum major, quick as a snake, shot his staff up in the air and caught it by the butt. The band fell silent, after which the drum major did some sort of routine with his staff and the band followed, this time getting in formations of circles while orchestrating the music, and then marching into different patterns. Each person was synced incredibly well, like an autonomous link of a chain. Soon it was over as the band marched away with a send-off of thunderous applause and cheering. After this, the real show began.

From the far end of the bridge, this time approached a large stage hundreds of metres long. It was a station with hundreds of wheels and powered by an engine. On it were miniature depictions of white Sanctum temples, black granite pyramids and scenery from around the world, some even scenes of war from verses of the *Tome*, with wax statues of soldiers. Around these scenes and the entire length of the platform were the priests, wearing either plain white cassocks or white vestments with turquoise stoles and maniples. They all smiled brightly and waved, with the people waving back at them.

As the platform kept zooming by, she didn't even notice what was coming towards the end, until she heard a jarring roar and flames sear through the sky. It was a white dragon floater, nearly fifty metres in length and powered through air turbines and mechanisms which filled its body and made it look like it was moving; twisting and turning like a serpent. It became stationary for a moment, and then shot up into the sky and swooped down, releasing flames. As it came down, the priests from below released the floats depicting the symbols of previous religions, which burned and perished in the flames.

The people cheered and clapped, appreciating their monumental historic moment. Reyn, however, felt dizzy, glancing towards Jack, who merely seemed indifferent. She just gazed at the road until the ordeal was over, and then finally, in the sky, with a noise like a thousand engines revving, and the intensity of thunder, manifested four massive sections of stadium bleachers, propelled with engines beneath it. They looked over the road from the sky, and each of them was nearly three storeys tall, with perhaps hundreds of seats for the lordly families in the top, while in a separately floored compartment at the bottom was seating for people who had possibly paid thousands and even millions to share a place in those airborne bleachers.

The people this time went completely berserk, jumping, cheering and throwing their stuff into the air. It was, however, 6pm, when the crowd went silent once again. Lord Rosendale made an announcement, asking for everyone to chant the verses respectfully, and wait for the Paragon and the main procession. People began chanting reverently, showing patience and subservience, indicating their longing to see the Paragon, showing that today they would pledge to be the best version of themselves, and the fact that a small glimpse of Paragon would change their lives forever. On and on they chanted, but there was no way Reyn was going to follow, not even in this hell, so she pulled Jack closer and mumbled under her breath, appearing that she had joined in, only to speak in his ear, "This is pretty freaking annoying…"

"Yeah, I threw up in my mouth a little," he mumbled back.

"Pretty much tough to believe that people actually believe these tales."

Jack started sniggering, until he broke almost too loudly into laughter and his body started shaking with it. "And even I used to spew this crap every day at school…" he finally said, attempting to quieten down.

"Yay for them after destroys everything of ours," she replied sardonically.

"I think honestly both sides are stupid."

What? she thought, surprised, as their eyes met. "What do you mean? Don't you support free will?"

"Ah, I do, but not everything else. You will have to tear this world apart to bring everything back, and to bring back everything, you will have to destroy every single thing about this world again, whether it is good or bad. What would we do if we manage to win? We can't rebuild anything, we can't bring back the culture. Is it still worth it for the sake of truth and free will to tear everything down?"

Reyn sighed, staring at her feet. "Sure, I guess, as long as we deal with this first, we can think about the rest..." She had started to feel nauseous and everything in the background grew distant. "Jack, I don't feel so good."

"Hold on, the main caravan will be here soon..." he distantly replied in the background.

The main procession came soon enough, carried by a massive Guren spacecraft of the military. It was white in colour, and shaped like a typical military jet, but much, much larger. The stage it carried was built in four storeys and designed like a castle; on the main stage stood the four mothers of mercy in their special white tunics. And on the one above were four staircases leading up to individual, separate precipices where stood four of the seven knights, and even from there, were two spiral staircases leading up to two more ledges where stood two more, and finally, on the top, there wasn't a stage but a round platform with the waving Sanctum flag and knight Rosendale himself. He was startling to see, as he smiled, plucked up the flag and waved it. Reyn felt her jaw drop and her heart racing just looking at his majestic white locks and a face so perfect that she was speechless. His white, glistening armour, trimmed with gold, really complemented his looks as well.

Finally, the four mothers walked ahead, towards the front of the stage. Two of them walked in the front, closer to each other, and two walked in the back, slightly farther apart. Then they stopped in their positions, before Angaria Storm, the mother ordained for the region of Sancta America, broke the formation and stepped forward, taking four precise steps, and raised her arms while the three mothers aligned themselves behind her to form a line. With the turning of gears and sounds of some clicks, the stairs retracted from the front of the stage and a special walkway opened up, stretching onto the road, where Angaria Storm walked and finally stopped near its end.

She let her arms drop and smiled, revealing a blinding set of teeth beneath as she swept her gaze over the crowd. The crowd gasped and bowed their heads in admiration; even Reyn felt charm-struck and dazzled. Many people started breaking into tears and fervently whispering the commandments of the *Tome*. Some even bawled in disbelief at viewing the godly deities with their own eyes. Somewhere in the crowd, a lady nearly fainted while bawling, "Forgive my sins, mother! Mother!" — which was just one of the many examples from a crowd of hundreds of thousands. Reyn honestly felt nauseated, and out of place.

How brainwashed were they? Their obsequiousness and zeal, was just beyond her. Was it this trait of the human beings, to unquestioningly obey what they're taught early on, which used to create wars? Maybe, but it wasn't as if Reyn knew any better.

"Jack..." she whispered ever so slightly once again, "I really can't..."; but it was so timid that it dissipated right from her lips.

And then Angaria raised a hand and announced, "Our children, cry not, for this is an auspicious occasion! Four hundred years ago, when our Lord felled the fowl religions of the heretics, he made us four, the pure mothers of love and healing, to counter the evil which maligns the feeble human minds! He saved us from the judgement day which we wrought by our own hands, and in turn gifted us this world which we live in. Yes, he rained fire upon this world, but not to harm us, no. It was to save us, unlike the God who promised to burn this world on his day of judgement. He truly revived this planet, and we, the fraction of the people alive, are the divine children altogether...!"

Reyn almost fainted, only for Jack to hold her back.

"Reyn... don't take it seriously..." but she just doubled over and threw up at her feet. Jack held her from falling, and no one noticed them, except for a lady who said, "Paragon bless you, girl."

As Jack was bent over, trying to comfort her, he felt the hair at the back of his neck crawling. He looked up, only to see people turning their heads towards them, and Angaria Storm grinned once again, pointing in their direction. "See… this occasion is of love — feel it — for the blessings which he gave you with the ability to bond with fellow humans…"

At that point, Jack flushed like blood, but Reyn just rose back up, disgruntled, wiping her mouth against her sleeve. Angaria once again resumed the sermon, and people ignored them as if nothing had happened at all. Except for an old lady, who giggled and patted Reyn's back. "You're a lucky young lady! Her holiness just noticed you!" For which Reyn just gritted her teeth, and did her best to ignore her.

Soon, her sermon was over, and the knights climbed down from the stairs, stopping at the main stage and making a wedge formation. The gimmicky walkway had retracted, replaced by the staircase once again. The knights summoned their horses, each especially bred and nearly eight feet tall. They then set up a tourney for the entertainment of the people. The crowd went especially insane when Knight Griffith's horse warped into an image of the space, oozing darkness like smoke and its body becoming a display of a million stars. Even its eyes went completely white.

Tristan Beckinsale, the heart-throb and perhaps the most beloved knight after Griffith, was also his opponent. He had side-shaved hair dyed pink, with a comely face and prominent cheekbones and jawline. His armour was also white, but this time trimmed with cyan enamel, the colour of his family crest. His iconic sword was in its sheath for the tourney, and was rumoured to be able to warp matter. His horse had also transformed, mimicking a nebula, and started emanating all sorts of colours as they went head to head. There were all sorts of scintillating lights, and displays of flashing weapons after that. Even in the sky, there were more Guren warships now, doing aerobatics that were nothing short of amazing.

Reyn, however, still felt too nauseous to enjoy the show. "When will Paragon show up…?" she grumbled, tucking at his sleeve.

Jack frowned. "Um, he doesn't, physically. There should be a flash of light presumably on that stage, lasting for a few seconds, and that will be it."

"Well, that's disappointing," she protested. "Can we leave already?"

"Yeah, okay, but maybe a little longer?" he tried to suggest.

She grunted under her breath, but nodded either way and decided to watch. Her only concern, even more so than her out-of-nowhere surging fever and nausea, was that Jack could end up doing something irrevocably reckless. Suddenly, she gasped. She couldn't explain it, but it felt like a premonitory chill. No one seemed to understand, though, even Jack. She tucked at him again, but he didn't listen.

"Psst!" she hissed, tugging his coat. "Something is happening. I feel the ground shaking!"

"What? Nothing is…" he managed to say, and then the crowd of thousands shifted around them like a tsunami, as they were all jolted off their balance and the ground shook, taken over by tremors and rumbling. Within a split second, she saw his expression turn from indifference to jaw-dropped, eyes wide in terror. All around them the people panicked, and in the distance across the area they saw smoke rise in the sky. The knights all glanced at each other in confusion.

"AT EASE, CITIZENS!" boomed the Arch-knight, but after a momentary relief, a deep thrumming shuddered the earth beneath them, like the rumble of an earthquake. The thrumming continued, and then it broke into a full-scale earthquake as people, now quite out of control, tried to get out from under and near buildings and structures. Within the chaos, she suddenly felt the rumble disappear beneath her feet.

"HEY!" wailed Jack, shaking her.

She gawked at him, eyes wide in confusion, and he pointed beneath them. They had clearly risen an inch or two above the ground, along with some people around them. The lady and a man behind her started glancing at their bodies and feet in surprise.

"I can't help it, Jack..." she whispered desperately. "My power seems to have taken over."

"Tch!" he replied in frustration, grabbing her arm and dragging her away. Their feet still didn't touch the ground, but now they were in a swarm where it would go unnoticed. Before they made it far enough, Jack turned and looked at the road once more, only for his pupils to constrict in terror.

"What?" she fretted. Looking back at the road, there was nothing out of the ordinary — well, other than the predicament that they were already in. But she felt him clutching her arm even harder as they tried to desperately make their way through. What did he see that terrified him even more than he was already? She wanted to ask, but there was no time.

It must have been more than an hour before they made their way out of the crowd of hundreds of thousands of people stretching over the streets of London in the parade zone. Finally, they made it through, gasping for air as the last road filled with the crowd of people was behind them.

"What did you see, Jack?" she whispered.

"I... Griffith saw us. It was a glare that I've never seen before... How did he know?"

Reyn had no idea how to respond. The best course of action would be to put this foolishness away and get back home before it was too late. Except, one of the screens live-streaming the parade near them suddenly broke into news as the anchor spoke. "The threat has been neutralised, citizens. Rumours are that the now long-believed-to-be-extinct organisation, Dark, has resurfaced and tried to ambush the parade and the general public…"

They both glanced at each other, stricken with terror and surprise. "Who… who could it be?" muttered Jack.

"Jack… I am sorry, but before we left, I called our friends for back-up…" she whispered, nearly breaking into tears.

He gazed at her with more disappointment than surprise. "Why?"

"Hey, you guys there!" squealed a childish voice. It was Lappy, to their astonishment, along with Maverick, Ashley, the twins and Kiara. "Why are they blaming it on us?"

"Huh… I don't know… but how did you guys find us?" asked Reyn, even more perplexed than before.

"We couldn't contact you, but then during the live stream we saw that one of the mothers literally pointed at you guys, so we knew where you were and took this route hoping to find you…" replied Zachary.

"Oh… so assuming from Lappy's question, you guys REALLY are not the cause of it, right?" Reyn asked.

"No," the group replied in unison.

"This can't be it then," said Jack coldly. "Who else could've caused that quake?"

Suddenly, from afar, a voice rang with cold apathy, “I am sorry, but just for the sake of what the world had to see right now, I cannot let you pass.” It was Knight Rosendale, charging towards them with quick strides, as the ground shook with each of his steps.

Shift of equilibrium

They lost their nerve in the moment and ran. Ashley, the twins and Lappy ran to their right; the twins, although being young military experts, did not have a tactical solution besides taking off to the right. Jack grunted and tried to step forward, but a bold, iron grip from Reyn clutched his arm and yanked him away with a force which felt enough to pull his arm out of the socket.

Maverick quickly stepped forward and raised his arms. Jack felt the invisible ripples fold like a whirlpool in the air as he splayed his hands and then scrunched them, concentrating the ripples. He smirked and snapped his palms open again, sending the ripples like a jet of wind in the Knight's direction. Everyone in the area felt the impact; Jack nearly staggered and fell, before Reyn's shield covered him. The other four hid behind a car, which rose in the air from the front briefly, before dropping down. The knight, however, stood at the heart of the explosion and cut through the burst of power like a knife through butter. He then clenched his fist and heaved the slightest of sighs, and then punched the road.

The asphalt split open a foot deep, and a trail of rocks jutted in Maverick's direction. It was so quick and powerful that before Maverick could jump away, the trail of jagged asphalt rose under him, twisting one of his feet and throwing him off-balance. He screamed and staggered back, falling on his butt. Jack clenched his teeth in blind yet unsure rage, and tried to move. But quick as lightning, Reyn was past him, her jet-black hair hitting him on the face. She had no offensive telekinetic power like Maverick, but her shield would blow anything away on impact.

The knight remained standing, with his eyebrows arched in surprise, as within a couple of seconds she had blazed through the distance, and was about to slam him with her shield. He raised his fists in defence as Reyn was about to pounce, and the knight's immovable stance rebounded the force back, crashing her on the road with a sickening thud.

He did not plough after her as she remained unmoving, but charged forward towards the four hiding behind the car. Lappy shrieked in terror, the twins jumped on the car's boot and then the bonnet, and escaped. Ashley tried to pull the extremely stubborn trigger of the discharge gun, but failed. Maverick once again stepped in, having a hand facing towards the floor to compensate for a twisted ankle; but as soon as the knight was close enough, he doubted his own defence and jumped back, taking Ashley with him.

Jack noticed the hesitation from the knight. He could have blown them to smithereens if he wanted to, yet he was completely in defence. Finally, Ashley emerged from behind Maverick and shot the lightning at the knight. The regulator on the rifle was set up at a full one million volts, and with a blinding flash which raised every single hair on Jack's body, she hit the knight's chest right in the centre. As Jack's vision cleared, momentarily hoping that a nearly point-blank distance for such a massive bolt surely would have halted the knight, it was utterly terrifying to see that he'd only staggered a step or two, with the red rose of the Rosendale family charred on the breastplate.

This time, the knight finally glanced over to Jack, frowning. It was as if he recognised a face but could not remember. Jack didn't know what he wanted, so he panicked, running backwards; but even with his quick strides, the knight was somehow too fast.

Reyn channelled her power through her limbs once again, wrapping her defensive power in and around her body, giving her temporary invulnerability. He tried to avoid her nonchalantly almost, but the burst of her physical attack sent him stumbling sideways, and then he was hit by a lightning bolt from Ashley, wave blasters from the twins and boulders torn out of the road from Maverick. All at once, he was finally stopped dead in his tracks and, amongst the barrage, a trickle of blood ran down his mouth.

For a faint moment perhaps, there was a glimmer of hope for them. But to Jack, it still seemed he was avoiding an active offence. The knight finally grunted, and punched the road with such a force, using his power of physicality, that it split in all directions.

Members of the group stumbled and fell. The twins and Ashley lost their guns, Lappy remained helpless, and Reyn was blown away, despite her shield's protection. They had no choice but to be at his mercy.

No matter what the knight's intentions were, Jack got up and scampered towards him. He had to take the chance. "We did not cause any of that. Look, something's been happening which none of us can explain. First, Allen's murder, then… then my…" — Jack couldn't muster the courage to take Alex's name — "and then at the parade!"

The knight stood there, looking at Jack, perplexed, yet in visible relief that he did not have to fight. "How can I believe you?"

"I know about you, I know about Ernaline."

The knight stood there frozen, as if receiving an answer which he never expected. He closed his eyes and sighed. "So, I believe you've dug down our history. Well then, this man you speak of — Allen — he was my father. What happened to him recently shouldn't have happened… it risks the peace of the past two centuries. I went around wondering if it was the Dark who did it, but it made no sense for them to do it now."

Everyone stood in shocked silence, especially the twins, Lappy and Ashley, who had no idea about their beloved Ernaline being involved with a sworn enemy, nor the fact that the man who seemed like a random murder victim in Jack's investigation was deeply connected to them, even before the cave was found. Even Jack himself would have never guessed that the mysterious general was… Allen, the person he knew.

Were the knight and Jack both originally set up with these murders connecting them? If yes, then it would mean that they both happened to be connected to Allen and murdering Alex was a way of drawing Jack there. It was like an attempt at sparking a war between the Dark and Sanctum through this.

Whatever the case, he needed answers regarding Alex's murderer. "Knight, I assume as someone as high up as you, do you have insight on who did that to my… friend?"

The knight sighed. "No, I know who could be behind all of this. I have been wondering for a while… but I cannot tell you."

The twins and Maverick swore at him, not giving a care about the consequences.

The knight shook his head. "No. Long ago, I would have killed you at the moment I appeared, but after all this time… knowing what the Sanctum has been doing, losing the glimmer of righteousness which

I once had in my eyes, I have not much faith left. But I will never lose my faith in Paragon. I… wouldn't be here without him. I am sorry for you children for being set up like this; perhaps you can escape now, and then never appear again. And as I spare you… I will have to disappear."

"Shit!" Maverick whispered, and everyone else glanced at each other guiltily, besides Jack and Reyn. What could it be? Maverick mumbled back, "I don't know if it is okay to tell you now… but you know what kept us hidden all this time? We had this seal called…"

"Seal of the Eight?"

"You know about it?"

"Yes. It was widely used for a long time, to hide resistance forces and power users during the war."

"Well… all of us here, the seven of us who left the cave… are part of the seal…"

The knight looked as if in both shock and surprise. "What a coincidence. The seal members in a place where I was set up to kill you. With so many of you out here, if even one of you dies, your protective aura will disappear, and due to the nature of your city, it will appear on our power-detecting radars instantly."

The group gasped. Reyn and Jack looked at each other, not knowing what else the others were hiding. They all dug into their phones, which could tell the status of their group members via a link connecting to their life source. Ashley dropped her phone, Lappy stood in shocked silence, Maverick swore up a storm. Kiara had passed away hours ago. She did not make it.

"The seal might break," said Griffith, entirely sensing their shock. "If one of you have perished, and almost all of you are this far away, then it will likely not hold up for long unless you return quickly."

Jack felt stunned. Lost. Days ago, everything went according to his plan; now he didn't even know what was happening. Lappy's communication device sputtered to life with a burst of static, and there was Lex's face bawling as he howled for help, "Guys! The Sanctum has invaded with their Gurens! There is no one in charge except for Van Vuren and Vanesse. The army is trying its best…" — and then it shut off. Last thing they heard was the deafening machine-gun rounds getting near his direction before the screen went out.

The knight sighed, as if having a long-winded debate ended within him. "I guess the pre-emptive strike is complete. Sanctum has destroyed the Dark."

The world spun and melted away in front of them. It made no sense. Zachary scooped up a rock and threw it at Jack in a rage. Ferrell held him back resignedly as it was too late now. "It's you! You bastards! Maverick and Jack. None of this would have happened if you had never joined!"

Jack only lolled his head, but Reyn snapped back bitterly, "Don't forget it was you guys who kidnapped both of them! If anything, blame goes on us for acting like this…"

Ashley chimed in, clutching for hope, "Guys, there didn't seem to be too many of Sanctum's forces yet. Our city can take it down; all we have to do is return and re-form another seal..."

The knight spoke up. "It is not so easy, child. Your city may not last today. But from tomorrow, you represent the Dark. Sanctum failed in their plan because I failed to kill you. Both of us are free from the pawns that our masters made us to be. Find Van Vuren, and tell him what happened. Tell him that I seek forgiveness for being the knight that crushed the Dark in the second century war. And yes, your Elders have hidden much from you," he said, looking specifically in Jack and Maverick's direction. "Farewell. The citadel is empty and unguarded."

He walked away, while his armour disappeared, leaving a leather jacket and blue denims beneath; and so, after some distance, he disappeared altogether, leaving the road miraculously fixed behind him. He had officially ceased being the Arch-knight of the world.

All they could do now was to stand shaking at the predicament. Lappy frantically tried to dial in his device, to be told that the city was okay with minimum casualties, and that they still had a home to return to. The device didn't respond, but a *NightScythe* warped into existence near them. From within stepped Van Vuren, a stream of tears running down his face as in his arms he held Kiara's body.

Humanity strikes back

"Do any of you know what you have done?" cried Van Vuren. No one had an answer, or an excuse. Anything that contributed even a hair's breadth to this destruction was inexcusable. None of them spoke. It was too quick and unreal to be grasped, let alone be enough for them to come to terms with it and shed a tear.

For a moment Van Vuren remained unmoving, like an idol. He had seen more than a fair bit in his lifespan of two hundred and so years; the rebellious ghetto of the Colombian branch of Dark he grew up in. The comrades he had, the fellow horsemen he had; Grim, Alward Savage, Ernaline Tora. All dead in their war for freedom, to create a peaceful homeland that later became the city of the Dark. To him even the second century war seemed such a far event, the figures of horsemen but ancient and long gone for him.

At times he did despise them that their flame went out in their glorious dreams of a free world where no one would have to live under tyranny. Yet he was the only one remaining. The cautious one, the one believed to be the weaker and the indecisive one. Was being realistic and wanting to salvage what they already had really something to be considered weak? Or was it them, his friends, and the hundreds of thousands of people of the old armies that couldn't last the war? In the end, who was it to see the dream child of the horsemen grow? Who was it that nurtured the city? Yet it was only him that lived long enough. Long enough to see even that dream-child die.

Truth be told, the peace of nearly two hundred years in the cave had made his passion cold and content inside. He had already saved the people; there was no need to drag them into the terror he had seen in the past. Yet, these six children in front of him, that he raised like his own, led up to this. He couldn't blame them; he couldn't blame Jack or Maverick, given their real past, which he knew. He could blame himself for not telling them; but no, it was the youth, surging within them with naivety and anger.

Before anyone could speak, he quickly got the group to board *NightScythe*. He placed Kiara's body peacefully in the cryogenerator at the back of the ship, and then warped the ship out of London to somewhere else over an ocean.

"I am sure… the place is still saved, right?" he heard a feeble voice coming from the deck while he operated the cockpit. It was Jack, the only one who could keep his wits together.

"No. They found the house and our energy signal right as the seal broke, which their Guren used to teleport inside the cave. I used this *NightScythe* to teleport out and destroy the house, so they shouldn't be able to find the cave again. But that's just to stop them from exploiting our technology and secrets. It was too late… too late to save all the people. We sent out as many as we could with the rest of our ships, hoping that they would find protection in the region of Scythe," he replied, only a part of him with barely any hint of hope.

He could hear cries, but it was the truth. For now, for them right there, the Dark was gone. He did not have rage in him to keep going in a cycle that would never end, but he did not know what to do yet.

When he went back to the deck, Maverick had to ask one thing, "Kiara… she was with Fr…?"

Van Vuren shook his head. "Fred is the one who lured you. I do know what made him sell us out after our century of trust, but whomever it is, will answer for it."

An air of guilt blanketed the room as Van Vuren finished. Maverick stared at his feet, not daring to move an inch. They all felt ashamed for being so naïve and reckless, only now realising the consequences of their actions.

It was Jack who had to speak up. "The Arch-knight has given up on the Sanctum. He told us the citadel is completely empty and unguarded due to the parade."

"What rubbish…" Van Vuren mumbled, but the earnest look on their faces, didn't lie. It was then he snapped, clenched his teeth, knowing what he had to do.

"What did he say before leaving?" he demanded, once again in his calm yet powerful voice, this time fuelled with conviction.

"That it is empty and unguarded…"

"That's enough." He knew what he had to do. Off with the peace that he had sold his conscience for. The Van Vuren, the one known to be the strategist back in the second war, had returned. Even if it was a ploy by Paragon to lure them there, he knew exactly what he had to do.

Over at the sea, the night was completely dark, clouded and windy. The water was becoming reckless beneath them; from crawling in small waves to speeding up with the wind. He let the group grieve, but soon called them out for the briefing. He couldn't let sorrow gobble up their rage in this adverse time.

In front of him, on a square wooden table in the middle of the *NightScythe*'s deck was the holograph of the citadel's structure. It was a floating chunk of land in the air, shaped very much like an iceberg on the bottom. On the top, it primarily had two hills next to each other, the right one being slightly tilted towards the back. On the hills were two giant obsidian pyramidal palaces with uneven bases merging with the hills. On the left hill, beneath the obsidian palace, there were windows carved into the rock wall, like an ancient fortress. The hill on the right was much wider, stretching even farther to its side, eventually splitting into two sections and having a valley in between. On both these hills, besides the black obsidian palaces, were three plasma-shooting spires. The three spires on the left were aided with defensive turrets, which were located at the bottom of the hill, near the boundary.

Finally, he began his briefing. "Okay, as you can see, towards the left side of the land you have these gigantic turrets to shoot down the enemy. These can obviously rotate, but cannot cover the right side of the citadel; while the right side doesn't have any, because of the uneven terrain and not having a clear boundary to install a line of defence. However, to compensate, either sides of these palaces have three spires. Each of these spires shoot plasma beams, made from the deadliest and the rarest of the plasma generators. You see how this right hill is also slightly taller, as well as slanting down farther to the right? This makes an advantageous shot for the spires on the right to not only take down airborne enemy from all sides, but also to take an easy shot downwards, right towards the earth from the sky."

"But then how do we beat them?" Jack asked, gaping at him quizzically.

"Lack of weakness does not assure invulnerability. In fact, it is precisely their automated system which we can manipulate. Here..." — he pointed towards the land on the left of the citadel — "If you can distract from the left, the turrets will aim and shoot you in that direction. For this, we will release our position on a selected radius, baiting a nearby Guren searching for us. As soon as they teleport here, we will teleport in the air at the left side of the citadel. The Guren will do the same as it always does, and it will follow without knowing our destination. But as soon as we get there, the turrets at that distance won't know friend from enemy, and will start shooting. It is a very risky move for us, but a Guren is a much larger target than we, so it will distract while we can escape. This will be the duty of the other *NightScythe* hovering beside us right now. Now for the spires. I told you that they can handle it in the air, and shoot towards the earth as they're on the hill, but they can't shoot within the citadel itself. For this, we will teleport right beneath the citadel, and using jetpacks we will climb up from the right. While the Guren is being shot on the left, a few of our elite members will infiltrate the Guren and open its energy field so the turrets will be locked in a loop and will keep firing at it. Then the rest of the members can use jetpacks and climb up from the left. All we have to do then is find the source of the aethernet, hack it, and telecast the real historic events to the minds of the people across the world via the tracking chip in their spine."

As he briefed, his voice boomed over the speaker in the *NightScythe* beside them. The people from there had come towards the window, looking over to the eight of them across the air. The kids went to the window and waved. They were all soldiers, nearly a hundred and fifty of them wearing their blue military vests and deep green suits. Many waved back passionately as streams of tears ran down their faces.

"So, what's our duty? Which one will we be split in?" asked Reyn, still looking at the soldiers through the window.

"All of you will remain here and follow me," replied Van Vuren in an assuring tone. He then turned, looking towards the other ship. "All of us have trained our lives for this day. To throw our dreams and lives away in a cry for freedom." He raised a fist in the air, and then thundered, "Soldiers! Do you not wish to create a day where our children do not have to live in fear any more?"

They raised their fists in the air and commenced a war cry.

"SOLDIERS! DID YOU NOT PLEDGE TO THROW YOUR LIVES AWAY FOR THE DAY WHEN WE FINALLY SET THE WORLD FREE?"

The soldiers screamed and cheered, and the *NightScythe*s revved up. Van entered the cockpit and selected a radius on the radar on the control panel to release the signal. Within moments, a Guren teleported near them.

And then the other *NightScythe* teleported, successfully taking the locked Guren with it. Moments later, they followed, as a familiar feeling of swirling through a needle's hole and being stretched into a string welcomed him.

They were directly beneath the citadel, casting its dark, ominous shadow over them. As soon as they glanced to the left, the turrets had landed a couple of hits at the other *NightScythe*, piercing through its armour in places. But the bait did its work; the Guren followed and eclipsed the ship, taking the majority of the hits.

The elite soldiers risked their lives through opening fire from the turrets, grappling to the Guren from underneath and blasting their way through the hatch. They cleared the lightly guarded deck, and then enabled the energy shield. After which, they quickly slid down with their grapplers back to the *NightScythe*, and moved it under the citadel, where it was safely free from fire.

Nearly all the soldiers could now be dispatched and fly up via jetpack. Van Vuren almost gave the signal for the kids to activate their own when their speaker triggered.

"Van, we are unable to open the hatch again. It is damaged from the turret fire. Do you copy?" came the message from the other ship.

"I am coming," he replied, and prepared to take off, but Ferrell stopped him.

"Let us two go…"

"No, you have to get on the top…"

"No, Van. We can't risk you, even if it is minimal. You guide all these nuts to the top, and we will be up there with the rest of the squad."

Van seemed apprehensive, but Ferrell continued, "You're commanding; if something happens, then what? The commander needs to get on the top and lead. If you fold up and die down there, we will be as good as useless. We've never fought our own battle, let alone a war." Ferrell then jumped, followed by his brother Zachary.

Van smiled, feeling his eyes water. They really had made it. The little twins he remembered running around in their overalls — Ferrell being the cooler and understanding one and Zachary the impulsive and the cheerful one — they had finally grown up enough to tell him off.

He shook his tears off, and nodded to the rest of them. They jumped from the hatch, following him, and activated their white jetpacks, each of which weighed about thirty kilograms. They sliced through the air, heading towards the right side of the citadel. The distance went by in a moment as his hand tapped the edge and they then landed. They had made it. This was his second attempt in life going up against the citadel, but this time there wasn't an army to stop them.

The valley between the hills was absolutely breath-taking; it had multiple resorts of its own and miniature waterfalls cascading in between the cliffs. It had giant redwood trees approximately sixty metres or so, holding vast, interconnected tree houses. At the very bottom was a dense, lush area and the main waterfall pooling into one of the cleanest streams he'd ever seen.

But now wasn't the time to admire. He gestured the kids around him to stay together and looked up to the three black spires at the top of the slanting hill. He then pulled his pistol out and shot at it. The spires quickly sensed it, as the revolving lens at its apex spun and stopped somewhere in their direction. The lens glowed purple and concentrated as if locking up on them, but could not do anything. The angle didn't allow it to shoot within the range of the citadel itself.

"Phew!" he sighed, and then nodded for them to follow; while the lens, otherwise unknowing of their presence, spun away back to its usual position. He still stepped wearily and used his power; the ripples detected any nearby traps or electronic weaponry and sensors. So far, so good; nothing seemed to be upsetting.

Soon, as they made their way beside the right hill, the left side of the citadel boundary came into view, which was lined with a massive artillery of turrets installed into towers nearly ten metres tall. Finally, faces started appearing over the boundary, as the people landed and dusted their clothes off. Some hugged and cheered. Some remained vigilant. It was lively. It was a successful gambit. But there was much to do, and so he shot a flare into the sky to signal that they had made it as well.

Their members on the left saw the signal and broke into smiles. Finally, in the rear appeared the twins, stumbling with the weight of their jetpacks. He was relieved immensely to see them. He only smiled back coolly, but his brows remained concentrated. No matter the turbulence of emotions he went through this day, the people only saw his wise, unchanging veneer. If he could drop it, he'd be grinning broadly for this fleeting moment, but his expression remained calculating and knowing. It knew better than excitement and impulses at his age. In fact, he wondered if his face, an earthen mask, ever felt the same emotions which his mind deeply otherwise felt inside.

He nodded to them; they started assembling, dispatching their jetpacks and then equipping their lightning-discharge rifles and strapping their wave blasters closely on their back. The formal leaders took the command and the soldiers started following in files. The turrets kept firing at the Guren below, but something went awry.

One of the turrets that they edged by a bit too close sensed them. It stopped firing. They didn't consider that it could prioritise the enemy in the closest range. And then the loop broke, the turrets spun and aimed in their direction, and then fired.

Massive projectiles from a dozen directions were shot, tearing some people to bits. Faces which were smiling a moment ago, blew and splashed on the floor.

"RUN!" he thundered, and the files broke into disarray, dodging and hiding right beneath the turrets, where they couldn't aim vertically down enough. Many were quick, made their way through the line of artillery and ran towards the group as turrets were preoccupied.

Van focused all his power, shooting the steel bearings from his pistol with such a force that they exploded on impact with the turrets. Within seconds he took them all down in a fit of rage. The kids behind him and the ones who escaped also shot at them, trying desperately to take them down. Thankfully, there were not many casualties with the quick response.

But, during the chaos, he couldn't track which soldiers escaped. Even so, during the disarray and his effort to take the turrets down, his eyes searched for the twins. With their panicked attempt to escape the firing while they were so close to the ledge, he saw both — Zachary and Ferrell — their faces frozen in terror as they fell over the edge behind them without their jetpacks.

Rustle

They were in the office building, sandwiched between the fortress on the left hill and the hill on the right. The steel-blue tiles glared under the constant, relentless lights of the corridor. The corridor which stretched up to everywhere and nowhere. They had split up after entering the main building; the plan was to find the control room which monitored the aethernet.

But for all that seemed like an eternity to Jack, he had been going in rounds; corridors lined with offices and rooms which were firmly locked, had no labels, and upon opening felt like the most generic combinations of work environments. Maybe their group should have infiltrated some other part of the citadel; but, as it turned out, this was where the office area, or an official area, seemed to be.

He had been grouped with Maverick, Ashley, Reyn and Lappy, all of whom split up to scrounge through the corridors quickly. The twins were probably with the other soldiers after the turret ordeal, but Jack didn't know where.

After running relentlessly for about fifteen minutes, he came back to the exact office he had unlocked in the beginning, with a blue office chair and a table immediately beside the door, and an adjacent table with a red office chair. He had run in a circle.

He addressed the group through the microphone in his ear, "Guys, rendezvous at the receptionist's desk; we're running in circles."

Within minutes, they were all at the receptionist desk, wondering where in this bland, nameless set of doors they would find anything valuable.

"I think we should go check the palaces or something. I don't think anything is here at all. Maybe this place is just a distraction," said Ashley, scratching her head.

"No, I don't think so. There must be something of importance to be held, if this place is so elusive…" Maverick argued, while glancing at Jack for support.

"I think I know what this place could be. It is designed like a labyrinth that easily takes us back to where we start from," Jack answered, glancing around at his surroundings.

"Then we blow these walls out. It won't be a labyrinth if we destroy it."

And so they did. They found their guns and started blowing the doors and walls out. There was no further time wasted spent musing or chattering. Soon enough, they saw through the corridors and nooks that not only led them nowhere but connected back to the original path. Only through their rampage, did they suddenly stumble across a massive, hunkering steel gate, about three metres tall and two metres wide. Beside it was a security scanner, a blank turquoise screen which could detect the official personnel. Since none of them had anything which they could use for a faux scan, there wasn't much else to do except for Maverick's solution, which was to shoot the gate. He shot the door with lightning, but it didn't even scorch the door. He then removed his backpack, conjured the grenade launcher off the holster, and shot. Everyone squealed and ran back, yet the door remained adamant, despite the floor beneath getting scorched and blown out.

"Maverick, stop. Forget the door; we don't need to blow the door up if you can blow up the wall, am I right?" said Jack.

His eyebrows shot up with realisation, and then he shot at the wall. Still nothing. Frustratingly, he shot at the scanner itself, but despite seeming delicate, it remained unyielding.

"Wait, no! Don't destroy the scanner! If we do that, we might as well be permanently stuck!" cried Lappy, pushing Maverick before he could shoot another grenade.

"All right then, go ahead, do some of your digital trickery, but not before I try this out," Maverick responded, raising his arms and snapping his palms open. The burst of ripples and the gust of wind blew everyone away. Reyn stood unscathed, shielding Jack and Ashley near her. Maverick knocked himself out with the force of his own attack, his head hitting the marble with a dull crack.

"As expected..." mumbled Lappy. "Now, if you're all calmed, you've realised that this isn't an ordinary gate. It is combined with power to not only be invulnerable against blunt force but also to absorb your power, which is why none of you could budge it," he said, and then moved in closer to the lock for inspection. "I can't do anything with this, as we can't open it or do anything to the screen."

"Well, what then? We sit here and cry ourselves to sleep?" Maverick sneered, still clutching his head.

"Well, no, we will use your power, but this time with my brains..." he said, winking, only to be met by awkward stares. "Well, anyway, use your power like water and let it seep into the scanner through its edges."

Maverick nodded and stood up, scrunching his fingers, aiming them towards the lock as if strings were attached to each of them. Then he closed his eyes and moved his fingers slightly, trying to find his way in through the microscopic edges between the turquoise screen and the box surrounding it. "I can't, dammit, there's literally no space; it's like it's completely ripple-proof and won't let me in," he said, grunting.

"Keep trying," encouraged Lappy. And so Maverick did. With a few more tries, he sighed nervously and nodded his head.

"All right then, wrap your power around the panel itself and rip it off the wall. I will handle the wires and the programming within," Lappy instructed affirmatively.

The panel came off the wall, the pretty turquoise screen hitting the floor abruptly with a clank. Lappy immediately got to work, fidgeting with the programming and rendering the scanner useless. With some more tinkering, a red light amidst the jumble of circuits blinked, and the door opened.

They were now within the lowest floor of the fortress etched into the left hill, which was connected to the office. The interior was completely different, something yet unseen, as it was unlike the expensively furnished environment of the citadel. It had a simple, grey-plastered floor with no alluring quality. The windows on the left looking out of the fortress were large, unshapely, and haphazardly carved into the hill, although its edges were smoothed out.

"What is this place?" whispered Lappy.

"This is where the knights live, however many hundreds of them there are," said Jack.

"So, what do we do now?" asked Maverick, placing his hand on Jack's shoulder. Jack glanced around him; it wasn't just Maverick, but everyone that was looking up to him. They had no idea of this place, they hadn't lived in this world, and they expected him to lead them on as if he knew this place better than them from within.

"Well, from the look of the floor and the windows, we have hundreds of rooms to inspect. We do not have time for that. Try searching for rooms of generals, lieutenants, sergeants — anyone of importance, in fact. But above all, keep an eye out for the rooms of the seven main knights. You, Lappy and Reyn, go explore the middle floors together. Maverick and I will split the upper floors. Ashley, you… you stay on this ground level and communicate with Van Vuren." As he finished, Ashley's curious hazel green eyes went from affirmative and ready to disappointed and sad.

"Why me? I want to help, too — I can come with you. You need help, so I will help. You can't be by yourself like Maverick…"

"Ashley," he said, reassuringly squeezing her hand, "you are the only healer, I think, in our entire combined garrison. Should anything bad happen to our soldiers, the bottom floor is the perfect place for you to rush out as quickly as possible. Taking you with me or filling your hands up will only complicate things. This way, even if it's one of us who gets injured, we four can recuperate on the floors above and bring the patient to you."

She frowned for a moment or two, and then nodded reluctantly. Reyn still seemed concerned, but Jack wasn't having it.

"No," he replied with calm, unrelenting certainty. "The top floor is where the Arch-knight's room should be. I think if anyone… I want to be the one to see what the fuss is about."

And that was that. They split and started searching their own floors. So far, through the microphones, good news was starting to break. The Sanctum was largely unaware as the parade was moving from London to another city for the next day. Even in the night, the army wasn't returning. On palaces above, people had found a plethora of weapons from the lordly rooms. They had found a way of permanently disabling the spires and the turrets. They had even disabled any outgoing communication, so no one could report them for intrusion, even if they were somewhere inside.

All of that was in his reality. The reality he thought had permanently gone dark. He quickly kicked or shot down the doors, to find that, unlike the exterior, the rooms were extravagant and usually a mess, littered with liquor, equipment and their weapons. For a moment or two, he was tempted to try the armour which they had left sprawling messily in some of the rooms, or pick up weapons. But either way, he resisted and kept walking. The discharge gun felt heavy in his hand, with what felt to him like a slight buzz form, its core waiting to be unleashed. The regulator on the side was set on a default fifty thousand volts, which he couldn't increase because of having no power to channel into the rifle. But that was enough to kill or disable anyone at this short range. He found the pair of coated spectacles from his coat pocket and strapped it to his head so he wouldn't be blinded by the flash, and then kept moving.

So far, half the floor was scavenged through, with nothing conspicuous enough. Soon, he could take the spiral staircase at the far end of the corridor and ascend to the final floor, the floor which had only one room — the Arch-knight's room. He felt blood rushing through his veins, and adrenaline pumping in anticipation. He thought of the moment when the knight had dissipated in front of them while he walked away. He was drawn to the knight, knowing the truth which he had suffered through his inescapable fate. His eyes watered up as suddenly Alex's face appeared in his mind.

"No!" He snapped back and shook his head. There was no time to ponder, and so he routinely kicked the last door, gawked in, and decided to ignore the rest of the corridor for the most part and head towards the top floor. So far, so good; everything was eerily calm and going well for their whole intrusion. The day of freedom was here…

A very faint whisper — no, a rustle — too hoarse, like screeching nails against a chalkboard, reached his ears. He jumped back and spun to his left, where he thought the noise came from… It was empty. His ears perked up to listen closely once again, but nothing followed. It was probably the wind, as, after all, the fortress was hewn into the mountain, splitting up the wind at its haphazardly carved windows.

He sighed, and decided to check all the rooms. The creak of the door, the distant whirls of the wind, and yet the eeriness of the silence after that noise felt more prominent. More doors were kicked down, more creaking noise was heard, and more tiringly normal images were met — and yet, somehow, the creak and the whirls became more distant with each step towards the end of the corridor. It was as if the silence ate the noise. Thick and tangible, swallowing the natural sounds.

As he convinced himself of just being paranoid and decided to move forward, the ringing of silence also disappeared. He frowned; what was that feeling? Even the ringing was gone... had he lost his hearing? He gasped, but heard nothing; he almost panicked, wanting to scream, but slicing through the thick deafness followed a specific noise. A wet, smothered sound, slopping away in one of the unchecked rooms. He felt his hair prickle up, so he clutched his gun and ran towards the rooms where he thought he heard it. He kicked the doors down and walked inside, but there was nothing there, except for a slight, pinkish residue on the white floor. It wasn't like paint, nor did it seem like blood. It was just volatile, disappearing quickly. What could it be? Probably the knights fooling around...

Something latched itself on his thigh. He screamed, panicking, and fell over a knight's bed. He grabbed his legs, only to hear the microphone come alive. "Jack? Jack? Do you copy?"

"Yeah! I mean, yes. On the seventh-floor fortress, I copy."

"It's Van Vuren here. Report from the palaces: no control room of sorts found. Nothing of importance reported yet from the fortress team. Have you found anything?"

"Nothing yet; heading towards final floor — the Arch-knight's room."

"Relay on sight when you reach the room, over."

Jack nodded to himself and strode towards the staircase, quickly getting over any paranormal thoughts. He kept his rifle clutched in his left hand while climbing up the spiral staircase as quickly as possible. His vision finally broke the surface to see a corridor completely dark, save for the bluish hue of the moonlit sky. But the room was open, spilling out a pool of white light in the middle of the corridor.

Someone's there already? he thought; but it couldn't be the case. The flashlight in the gun didn't work, so he fumbled for the torch in his pocket, but his hands were full and it could be anywhere in his coat. He moved forward instead, not liking the feeling of the dark, spiralling staircase lurking right behind him. A chill breeze passed through the window, piercing his skin. After all, he was higher up the hill, and the floor was vulnerable to the weather.

The fear took over and he broke into a sprint towards the room, not stopping until he was outside, sweating and glancing towards the staircase, which was completely shrouded in blackness from this distance. He breathed deeply and spoke.

"Hi, it's Jack; do you copy? I have found the Arch-knight's room." His own voice reverberated, becoming louder and distorted like a demonic chant. After which, his microphone did not respond.

He swore loudly, losing his only means of communication due to some stupid technical fault. He swallowed the knot in his throat and marched forward, stepping towards the room. Just a quick check and he could run away to report back.

The room was… mundane, unexciting and normal. There was a bed covered with a blue blanket, and on the two tables on either side were stacks of books. He carefully edged towards the table and picked up one of the books. Some were on old history; some were about science, and some were written in an ancient language he couldn't understand.

He thumped the heavy book down, back to the stack on the table, and glanced around the room. It really was ordinary, except for the view it had from the fortress window. He did see, however, a slightly ajar cupboard, etched into the wall. It was a lumbering hunk of wood and old fashioned. He edged towards it cautiously and opened it. Nothing but plush robes inside and some ordinary clothes like denims and jackets, and beneath them, spread lazily, was a bunch of train tickets on a shelf.

He sighed and shut the cupboard, glancing around the room. There was nothing else of interest. But he couldn't leave. Something still felt quite strange to him. Either way, he threw off the feelings and headed towards the door.

Smack. From the quietness of the room came a loud, heavy, wet smack somewhere against the wall. He swung back: the noise came from a door inside a small alcove at the back of the room, hidden beside a mirror table. He kicked it open and brought his gun forward, ready to shoot.

It wasn't a restroom, but a passage. He shouted a threat to anyone lurking in the darkness. There was no response. He gritted his teeth in irritation, and shot the lightning through the darkness. It was blinding in this tiny spot, but he shut his eyes and kept firing, grunting in anger each time. After using up nearly half of the charge, he stopped, shaking with fear. The flashes of light had only made one thing clear: that this was no ordinary passage. In fact, there was a vast, looming space within. As his vision cleared, he wiped his forehead with his sleeve and crouched forward, and then rummaged for the light in his pocket once again. He finally found it, and then switched it open.

There were two tunnels in a cave system leading off to somewhere. He shed the light to either side, and towards the right the cave stretched openly for some distance. He did not like caves. They felt of dust and death. He tried heading back from the hole, until he saw something written on the wall, above and beside it. It was trailing ink from words written in red and black: "Do not approach the creepy Lord."

"What the actual…?" Jack swore a little too loudly. Was this written by the knight? It felt unlikely. But whoever this creepy lord was, he probably resided in the hell leading through these two tunnels. Jack bit his lip. Should he report this back or continue forward by himself? He knew reporting was better; he couldn't disappear into this mess, leaving them unaware of a missing member. But if he did, he'd lose the trail of the thing that caused that sound. He'd already wasted enough time. So he made up his mind, and moved forward; all he had to do was pick his poison and go either left or right.

It could have been only minutes, but it felt like hours went by as he moved through the dark, ominous tunnels. They seemed to be a natural formation, sometimes haphazardly formed, jagged on the floor and the overall shape, and other times they were unnaturally smooth. Sometimes he encountered stalagmites of minerals glimmering under his light. Often, the water dripped around these natural formations, forming small creeks. Yet for the most part the cave system was dry, chilling to the bones, and not very humid. He hated every moment of being in that place.

Eventually, he broke through a somewhat large, grey expanse. The wall on his left had several doors. They seemed to be some sort of rooms, in the middle of a creepy, lifeless cavern. He sighed and slung his discharge gun onto his back. It was too hefty and impractical to use. Had he encountered an enemy looming within the doors, his hands would have been too occupied to respond.

Instead, he unslung his sawn-off shotgun from his back, and quickly tied the torch to its barrel using the duct tape in his pocket. He prayed to whatever deity there was that he didn't encounter a human. He didn't even know if he could kill a person, much less with this monster in his hand which would turn a face into mush.

With the first door, he gripped the cold, silver lock, and abruptly shoved the door open. There was nothing within but a musty wooden table, some kitchenware on the counter at the back, and a large cobweb above it. This seemed like some very old watch place, he thought. The second door similarly had nothing. The third, the same. The fourth was going to be futile, after which only one remained. He twisted the lock, the door creaked open, releasing a cold jacket of air, and he felt his tailbone shattering as a black figure flew right onto his face and he crashed onto the jagged cave floor. He was flat on his back, panting and struggling to find his shotgun.

Just as his fingers felt the warm, sweaty butt of the gun, he heard the sounds of wet thumps running in his direction. Fast. There was the cold, hoarse rustle of the wind. The steps came nearer, the surroundings became silent except for the hoarse voice, and then it leapt. He fired in the air while he lay down, and in the flash, he saw a figure with a gaping mouth above him.

Whatever it was, it ran away and fell somewhere into the distance. Jack turned around once again, this time being careful that it did not circle him like it did previously. The natural echo of the cave returned: the trickle of water dripping, of his own breath, of creeks running and pebbles dropping. Is it dead? he thought, licking his lips and eyeing the torch. But he did not dare move, in case it tried pouncing on him. The sound of a running creek kept soothing his ears. Perhaps it was dead. Suddenly, in the beam of torch lighting the floor, he saw a flash of feet.

Quickly, he shone his torch in all directions. It was all but gone within moments. But he had a clue at least. His coat was splattered with the pinkish fluid left from its wound. The floor was a trail of the same fluid and its footprints which had splashed into it. It was a stingy, acidic and thoroughly unpleasant stench, like that of death. To his relief, though, at least now he had the footsteps to follow. He followed warily, keeping an ear for if things went too silent. Though, in his mind, he remembered a face within the flash… it had two ropes… no, two antennae. But that sounded absurd. Either way, he followed, walking in broad strides.

Soon enough, he thought he actually saw a light — or another, bigger cavern opening. This must be it. Although there was no sound being absorbed, he heard the familiar hoarse rustling getting closer. It seemed to be saying something, again and again, forming an echo like that of locusts. He gawked slightly around the corner, to see what the commotion was. After that, he was running. Running towards where he came from. He had always been bad at remembering paths. He did not reach the light, but he did reach a conclusion. Shaking and panting in the heart of a fairly narrow tunnel, he did not remember his way back.

High-octane rampage

Maverick screamed, raising his arms, moving them in a clockwise motion, and putting them towards the floor, boosting himself up. There were too many soldiers to face. But he wasn't afraid. Each moment he felt his grip improving over his power. Before he struggled to take two soldiers out, now he slashed a deep chasm into one through the armour, and blew him a hundred metres away as his blood gushed, trailing over the air. His fellows were similarly whipped aside. One even grotesquely had his guts slashed out before he was thrown away.

Everywhere around him was the buzz of electricity, and the silent danger of the wave blasters, but he did not care. He did not care that the Dark's own soldiers had terrified looks. He just crushed and slashed, pummelled and hammered any disgusting soldier in the white armour of the Sanctum. Their death only fuelled his thirst for vengeance.

The flow of soldiers started diminishing. The Dark's military took higher ground, shooting from the apex of the palaces and the fortress, using the turrets and the spires to attack Sanctum's Gurens. This defence made them near indestructible. But they had a small problem at hand: where did the soldiers come from, even when all communication was disabled? But there was no time to stop and address it. As he slowed down, briefly locking eyes with Van Vuren, which relayed that they had to deconstruct what just happened, a Guren teleported on the main citadel ground and ordinary knights started pouring out.

It did not last long, however; the overtaken spires shot their ruthless purple energy blast at it, and the fearsome warcraft came apart like the nimble shell of a boiled lobster. The knights, who had already poured out, deflected all the lightning, bullets and the wave blaster effects from the Dark's military. Their own mastery over the weapons was too strong, immediately firing lightning bolts and killing a couple of Dark members.

Maverick howled, putting his hands behind him and charging like a torpedo, uncaring of their weapons. Uncaring of how unprotected he was. He sliced through their formation. They turned towards him, but he launched himself into the air with a burst of ripples so strong that it blew the knights away. From the air, he curled his fingers up and gritted his teeth as the rage tore apart his own mind and covered his vision like a blanket of acid. He snapped open his palm, turning the knights inside out and blowing them to bits with a burst. With the remaining ones, he spread his arms open, and then clapped. The wall of ripples beat the knights into a pulp within their squelched armour.

He came down on the floor, cushioning his fall with the power. For the first time, he thought he saw a brief, proud smile on Van Vuren's face as his eyes moistened up. But Van wasted no time; he beckoned all the generals available to the spot, and then looked at Maverick with a firm, concentrated gaze. "You know what did just happen, right?"

Maverick frowned for a moment, making sense of the sudden attack. "We had disabled all the security... so naturally they shouldn't have known of any presence here."

"Exactly," said Van Vuren. "But it seems they are conditioned to get timely reports. Say, every hour their automated security must send a report back, even if nothing happens. We've been here for nearly five hours now; it is past midnight. They are beginning to suspect, hence a handful of troops were spared to investigate."

"So what are we supposed to do?"

"Best course of action for us is to enable the automated system once again, disable the sensors, and resend the timely reports manually."

"That's... that's genius! But what about this Guren and the soldiers we just killed?"

"That is the problem. Although with dozens of Guren around there for security, they are going to notice fast that their spared troops did not return. We have some time on our hands to quickly locate the control room before they become aware of their absence."

Interesting. He was right. But a small, and by small, the biggest problem remained. How were they going to find the control room? Maverick pursed his lips, thinking for something, and then finally asked, "Van… you old man, what should we do now?"

Van Vuren shook his head dismissively. "Jack has been missing for a bit now. Reyn went for him and has been missing as well. None of you five in the fortress had the sense to report this to us earlier. What should we do now? Well, the best course of action would be to find those two and hope we find the control room in the process."

"Can we not just find them and blow this citadel up using *NightScythe*s?" asked Maverick sheepishly.

"Ah, sure we can. Then we'll never know how they control the aethernet, the satellite, and the Sanctum would immediately be there to bite our arses," grumbled Mr Smith, stepping forward. He'd been awfully silent the whole mission, which was unusual for the normally drunk, fat master of physical combat.

"All right then, Maverick. You and I will go find Reyn and Jack. Mr Smith, I leave you in charge here. Should we fail to return within an hour, the best course of action for all of you is to rev up the *NightScythe*s and flee — escape to the Scythian region."

Lappy and Ashley voiced their opposition to that, but Van shut them down with a glare. Ashley gawked at Maverick with her innocence, but Maverick averted his gaze as if he hadn't seen. He knew that otherwise he'd never be able to resist her. But they weren't the only ones protesting: several of the soldiers stepped forward, speaking in opposition.

"Van, why do you care about that traitor boy? The attack on Dark wouldn't have happened without him. As for our girl, Reyn, you know she's our blood. We will help you find her," said one of them. He had a freckled, windswept face and a broken nose. Maverick knew who he was: he was Reyn's uncle. Someone who she didn't mention much, but he did resemble her father from the pictures he had seen.

Van almost softened momentarily, but replied in his stern voice, "Who is the traitor? You don't know who that boy is. He is as important to us as all of our soldiers here. So is your niece, obviously. But do you trust yourself, or me, the commander and the founder of the Dark, to bring her back safely?"

Maverick felt surprised. He didn't expect Van to be this blunt, but he really respected his sudden forthright reply. The uncle looked down with sad eyes and stepped back. A few people began speaking up once again, but Mr Smith raised his hand. "Stop. To each of you, being one of the masters, I can tell you that there are things that you do not know about."

And that was that. Next thing Maverick knew was that his boots echoed against the floor, as him and Van Vuren approached the top-most storey of the fortress. Their flashlights pierced the darkness, illuminating the spiral staircase ahead of them.

The doctor

Jack breathed heavily, his sweat rolling down his face in an endless stream. He was not afraid; he'd already had a nervous breakdown, and after that, all that was left to find his way back. Thankfully, as complex as the cave system seemed, he was able to work his way back. The deeper he went, the darker and more constricted it became. But, by following the tunnels that became airier, and altogether more spacious, he was able to traverse his way through. He had no idea how much time had been wasted. He had no idea if the world existed outside this maze any more; but what he did know, and was tired of, was the paranoia that the thing was still following him. Somehow, he couldn't get rid of the tingling that something was prowling behind him.

Soon enough, by keeping his nerves under control, he found the large cavern with the mass whispering and negotiated his way around it. His legs shivered just at the thought of the image he saw, but he did not dwell on it, lest it imprinted itself on his mind and messed with his already dwindling courage.

Though every lick of a billow and splash of the creek alarmed his senses, it wasn't until a bright beam of light suddenly illuminated the tunnel in which he was in that he jumped. Without thinking, he snapped, disappearing into a narrow crevice in the wall.

"Ah!" he heard a familiar voice scream. "THERE'S A WITCH DOWN HERE!" — followed by a horrifying blast of lightning bolt.

"STOP IT! You could've killed one of them!" Jack heard another familiar voice screaming back.

Suddenly, Jack squealed in happiness, jumping right back into sight. The wimpy figure at the end of the tunnel screamed and fell backwards, hitting its head with an empty thud.

"Jack!" called Van Vuren in relief.

Afterwards, they were headed back towards the cavern of the creatures. Maverick nudged at Jack doubtfully. "Come on, Jack, it can't be worse than what we've all seen..."

"It is."

"Come on, it can't be..."

The whirl of the hoarse whispers started becoming audible as they got closer. Maverick froze. Just the sheer eeriness of it was enough. "What is the sound?" he mused, his eyes widening in dread. He went ahead and gawked from the corner, before returning with a pale face. Van Vuren closed his eyes and sighed. "Ah, it is the angels, then."

"What?" both the boys asked in surprise.

"Jack, did you really see what they look like?"

"I couldn't. I have a phobia of things like that..." he replied ashamedly, but for the sake of the circumstances they were in, he had a good, long look around the corner. He heard them whisper the commandments from the *Tome* and its verses again and again, but within the nick of silver light streaming from the moonlit sky, he saw what they really looked like.

They were bipedal things... or people, brutally hunched and bent over, their limbs abnormally long and frail. From their eyes sprouted two long antennae-like whips, constantly moving and twitching around in the air. Their eye sockets were haphazardly busted open, and a stream of blood constantly ran down their faces like tears. It seemed to Jack that their hoarse whispers were a plea: the plea of a sycophant repeating its verses over and again, and crying a stream of blood while it was at it. Their skin was completely shrivelled and grey, webbed with grotesque black veins. One of them gazed in his direction, its mouth open, and its decaying and oddly chipped teeth snapping in his direction.

Jack pulled back, nearly puking. "I can't. They're like cockroaches..." — and then he thought of one of the verses in the *Tome* he'd read: the angels came not from the sky, but from the ground, where the corpses of the heretics were felled, or something like that. And then he felt a shiver down his spine, realising what those angels really were.

"So what should we do now?" whispered Maverick.

"Best to avoid them and move forward..."

"But where do we go? Do you know a way forward, Jack?"

Jack scratched his chin; he knew the way around it, but that led off to a hellish cluster of a cave system that he was lost in the first place.

"There!" whispered Van Vuren. "Look, at the far end of the cavern, there's a single tunnel there leading forward. Have you checked it yet, Jack?"

Jack shook his head: he hadn't. Van then decided that it was best to crouch their way through while the tunnel was still lit under the moonlight. And so they did; any minor noise went completely unheard in the echo of their chanting. It was all well, until Maverick dropped the flashlight. The skid of the plastic against the earth was the loudest sound Jack had ever heard in that moment. Even Van Vuren flinched in surprise, but thankfully the swarm of sycophants did not hear.

Gladly, they attempted to move forward, except that Maverick tried to regain the flashlight by using his power, and ended up blowing it in the process. The swarm momentarily froze in surprise, before the hundreds of antennae all swayed in their direction.

"RUN!" thundered Van Vuren, and so they did. Van hadn't been here before, but the boys still followed him, holding onto their dear lives. Once or twice, Van turned around, using his pistols to blow sycophants out. But it did no good. The swarm was overwhelming. Maverick tried blowing them away with concentrated ripples, but his power seemed to do nothing.

With abnormally long limbs, the sycophants pranced, outpacing them quicker than they could guess. When the swarm was near enough, Jack heard something like a hiss of a cockroach, and felt his back burning, before Van Vuren's firm grip grabbed him by the collar and hauled him into one of the adjoining passages. Van kept running, clutching Jack by the collar so his feet completely left the ground. Jack had a full view now, and it was not pleasant. The sycophants were opening their mouths wide, and throwing up two fleshy tubes out of their mouths which spat a green torrent of liquid. The liquid burned through the ground like it was cotton. Jack could only imagine what he'd be like had Van Vuren not pulled him back.

Despite the close escape, it quickly became clear enough that the sycophants were too fast for them. So they pulled into a narrower tunnel and Van Vuren shot the ceiling down to block the path. All three of them stopped, panting and holding their knees in relief.

"Let's wait for them to return, and then we can make our way back..." whispered Van Vuren very cautiously, making sure that the boys understood every word.

The three of them waited, forcing their ears to listen, to make sure that the footsteps of the harrowing whisperers had wandered away far enough. At first, standing near the walls and listening made it seem that the footsteps were receding, but after a while there was no distinction. They didn't seem to be going further. Had they just decided to stop? It sure seemed the case, which was bad enough. But hearing more closely, Jack realised that the footsteps hadn't just stopped midway; in fact, they weren't even coming from the same place. The noise had become a jumble because another horde was marching in their direction at the other end of the tunnel.

Van tucked at their sleeves, urging them to stick to the walls as closely as possible. The horde finally appeared in sight as their antennae ominously flitted through the air like tendrils of shadow. They stopped, and with no particular reasoning, they decided to step inside instead of moving forward, as if someone had just commanded them to.

Van Vuren zapped forward, and quick as lightning, shot at the stalactites above them. A couple of sycophants at the front immediately went down, and then, with brief pauses, he shot at the horde strategically, aiming and blowing heads off multiple sycophants at the same time. With three shots, he blew up nearly twelve of the creatures.

He stopped, calm and collected as ever, and dropped the steel bearings in the loading chamber, the muffled sound of which was oddly soothing. But the momentary relief was brief. Within seconds, a horde of footsteps trampled their way to them. And just like that, Van and Maverick blew up the blockaded entrance once again and escaped, while Jack, in a moment of panic, disappeared into the nearest crevice he saw.

He only remembered seeing a bunch of wailing faces that stopped and hissed at him, trying to spray him with their acidic discharge. Jack screamed, jamming his elbows and feet in the walls to either side until he was frantically climbing up. His clothes were burning, or maybe it was his skin. He didn't know.

Finally, he broke through somewhere, gasping for air, and a cold draught was welcomed by his lungs. His hair was wet and plastered on his face. He flipped the hair aside, screwing his eyes to drive out the wetness. It was him — him in the reflection of a stream running under him. Sallow-eyed, sunken and charred from the acidic fumes. He sat up, cupping the water in his palms, and washed his face over and over again. The coldness was soothing and the water was sweet, but feeling his skin with his fingers made it clear that this time it was no dirt that could simply be washed away.

Finally, he sighed, realising he was kneeling in the running stream, and the crevice he had just climbed from was right beside him. Somehow, there was a bluish light seeping into the chamber. He brought his arms forward, and saw the paleness exposed under the layer of burnt skin. The coat was gone, tattered and destroyed, so he remained in his tank top, which was also half-tattered, and jeans which were horribly gnawed through. The stream, he noticed, ran through a spacious corridor seemingly rather man-made, and deep within he knew this was where he was supposed to go.

He got up and walked, and kept walking, splashing through the water. Every footstep felt heavy, like having an anvil attached to it. He wasn't nauseous, but he felt like throwing up. He didn't know where he was headed once again, but he kept on.

A very faint scuttling of rock broke over the sound of the running creek, and two bony and cold, unforgiving hands gripped his arms. Jack reeled back, shoving the thing as hard as possible. The back of his head hit a sharp folding in the wall, which sent lightning into his eyes. He clutched his head and screamed, as his fingers tensed with the concussion. As he opened his eyes, he saw the surroundings swim. The lack of sight made him keep stepping to his left as fast as possible to avoid the thing as best he could. The splashes of another pair of feet kept following his, and finally, as he was able to make out his surroundings, he saw a stumbling figure trying to extend its arms towards him.

Once again, he pushed it back, but tripped backwards in the process. The sycophant followed and fell over him. Jack was petrified, as the jagged set of teeth in front of him revealed a mouth as dark as a gaping chasm, and from within followed a purple tongue, briefly moving in the air in a serpentine motion, drooling over him. It seemed to him that, for a moment, its jaw convulsed, trying to resist something, and then it set back into place as the sycophant began reciting the *Tome*'s verses.

But it wasn't done; a few words into the commandment, its jaw convulsed again and it started hissing as if fighting within itself. Jack, taking the opportunity, punted it hard in the stomach and got up, but this time taking his distance and adopting a fighting stance. The creature sporadically twitched, pulling at its own antennae, until, with a tremendous struggle, it slowed down and spoke in a very distantly human voice. "Sa-save me..."

WHAT? Jack internally screamed. Did he really hear it saying those words, or was it just an hallucination? The sycophant once again retched, but didn't throw up. Jack suspected that it had already torn its acidic glands out. It twitched a little more, as if spending every ounce of its willpower to retain its autonomy over its body, until all of its limbs snapped and it lunged towards Jack.

Within a flash, it was nailed onto the wall by its head as Jack instinctively shot a shard of rock at it. He exhaled heavily for a moment or two, staring at his hand, which was wet from going under the water and grabbing the shard. Did this hand just kill it — or her — by itself? Was this all real? he thought, and then he threw up. Its body was slumped over on the ground.

Unlike all others he had seen, it wasn't a gaunt, veiny skeleton barely covered with skin. In fact, under the pale sliver of moon breaking through, he definitely saw a pale, feminine body that was still quite human.

He shook off the thought and moved on, wondering how further messed up it could get before this was all over. The scene was once again replaced by constant darkness and feet splashing in the water. The tread wasn't endless like it seemed, as the tunnel finally led to a blue steel gate. A gate with the golden eye of the Sanctum, with the bleeding red tear.

The gate exploded in a thousand shards as Jack approached, too fast for him to even react. He stepped in, just to see the thousand shards pull up like iron filings and then re-form the gate behind him. They at least keep it fancy, huh? he mused.

Strutting through the corridors, the place was unremarkably monotonous and featureless; yellow-walled and dirty white-tiled, stacked randomly with crates, or with riggings heaving containers and other machinery which seemed to be properly secured.

He randomly found a beige overcoat lying on one of the stacks of crates, and although it felt like rubbing sandpaper over an open wound, he grudgingly put it over his body. Pity the guileless man who left it there; his life was probably changed forever after making his way into what was inside.

"In the hourly headline of the day…" he heard a familiar sound of News sprawling through a corridor which he was headed towards, so he rushed to the room where it presumably came from. The door was open, so he instantly caught what it really had to say: "The terrorisers of the Dark, who perpetrated yesterday's attack during the parade, were not only swiftly dealt with, but they were also justly destroyed once and for all!" And so were cued the live videos of the Dark being invaded by the Gurens while the people of the world were on the streets, cheering and rejoicing.

He shut the door and resumed walking numbly. If anything, this news was like the biggest practical joke he had ever seen. He could only imagine how a citizen of the Dark would feel watching this, but now wasn't the time for him to dwell on it. He kept walking, trying to inspect wherever he could.

As he got deeper into the compound, he often saw rows of freezers or a laboratory behind those locked doors. Trying to undo the locks and failing, he finally came upon one where it just seemed to open up. This screamed eeriness to him, but he walked in regardless. The room had a bunch of freezers lined up against either side of the room.

He picked a random one and tried to open it. He grabbed its handle and rotated the circular lock. It opened. From within, the icy smoke broke, briefly causing him to screw his eyes, while his hand found a random container. As the fog and the condensation over the glass container cleared, he saw it was a purple heart — gnarly and mutated, with veins protruding from it like roots. No thanks, he thought, and promptly placed it back, heading towards the only pathway available, through an exit on the other side of the room. At the end of that path was the last door, as unordinary as ever.

Your reality

The door opened up to gaping darkness, except for a smidgen of light lit by a row of computers. In the front of them, facing the screen in the middle, was a large, black chair. Jack waited a few moments, anticipating something springing forth from the darkness. Nothing happened.

The wheels creaked, and the chair moved ever so slightly away from the table. Then it swung, slowly rotating in Jack's direction. Upon it crouched a fairly underwhelming silhouette of the inhabitant, who was dwarfed by the enormous chair.

Jack clenched his fists. "Ar!"

The chair rocked in the gleam of those computers, and the silhouette of the man jumped from the chair, landing in the beam of light leaking from the doorway. "Hi!" he said in his whispery, dry voice.

"What is this place?" Jack asked, fairly confused by the man standing before him, who appeared to be a hunched-back, frail — a sort of teenage figure — in white sweater and black trousers. His messy, bedraggled hair fell over his eyes, both of which seemed to disappear into their dark, sunken sockets. His appearance was sort of unhinging for Jack to see, as if the closer he looked, the more he seemed like an ancient, reanimated corpse.

"This is the control station. I believe you've finally made it!" the man replied, smiling, but his eyes did not smile.

"Uh, okay, what're you doing here?" Jack inquired, still as perplexed as he was initially.

The man did not respond, staring back steadily, creeping out Jack as if he were staring at his own eyes in the mirror.

That is one REALLY weird guy, Jack thought. "SAY SOMETHING. Where's the boss?" He momentarily paused, considering the situation. "Now don't tell me you're the one?"

"I believe yes, you can call me Dillion."

Jack felt ridiculed, as if all the anger had been smacked out like the wind from him; but he did not know what to ask, or rather where could he even begin? "I don't have time for this. Are you putting up a show here for distraction?"

"You hurt me," the hunched man said, quipping like a child.

Jack sighed, trying to gain some semblance of the situation. "Let's do this again. You're telling me that you orchestrated everything leading up to the attack on Dark?"

"Yes, I suppose so."

Jack was mildly surprised by the response. This man did not look like he knew that his words carried any weight at all. "So, why'd you slaughter everyone…?" asked Jack, shaking with fury.

"You really mean to ask that? That's what we'd do as your enemy, right? Or should I say the Dark's enemy?"

"What do you mean?"

"I had… a long conversation with your friend Alex, and he told me that the very reason you'd entered the Dark was for your own personal curiosity. Later, you took their precious girl and left," said Dillion, shrugging nonchalantly.

"She chose to come with me."

"Oh, I know that she did, but you could've left without telling. Yet you took her along nonetheless, having your own personal gain at heart."

Jack made an impatient sound, choosing to ignore his rhetoric. "Why did you do that to Alex?"

"Ah, Alex and his family had to be the victims for this plot. I assure you, our mind-controlling technology is fairly sufficient. They did not suffer until the end."

Jack howled in fury, finally having the rage consuming the better of him. He rushed at the man, only to be dodged as the man sprung clumsily and disappeared within the darkness. Jack grunted with frustration. "And you dared teach me about the truth?"

"Heh, heh, heh… I do not twist the truth, I merely present it so it seems obvious to you," the voice replied.

Jack smiled, hearing the direction of the voice nearby, and lunged.

"WAIT!" shrieked the voice from the darkness. "At least don't beat me until you see what I do here." He ran towards the wall next to the door, searching for something. Finally, under the ambiguous lighting, Jack could make out an outline of a control panel built into the wall. The man prised it open, and with a heavy screech of a lever being pulled, the lights on the roof sparked to life, illuminating the lab row by row. The man looked down, blushing away as the light brought him forth into view. "Well… welcome to my clandestine haven."

The laboratory behind him was within full view now. It was less a laboratory and more of a factory… a literal human factory with an assembly line.

From their vantage point, they stood about a storey higher, and below them stretched a vast, cold hell, in the middle of which was the conveyer belt, starting under them and stretching all the way to the end of the enormous lab before it looped back.

The belt was filled with naked, unconscious humans strapped to it, each of whom was implanted with four pipes feeding into their chest, two on either side, and a cluster of smaller pipes feeding into their various organs, and from the back into their spine. Both the male and female victims had gone under surgery.

And this was just the victims on the conveyer belt. To either side of the assembly line were two columns of tall, vertical glass tanks filled with greenish liquid, in which there were more victims floating and plugged in with breathing aids. There were coils of pipes writhing around the columns and feeding into each of the tanks. It was where these victims were growing, starting to show signs and transforming into the sycophants. Some were just beginning to grow the antennae, while their bodies became more shrivelled and their limbs elongated.

The ones who were nearly fully transformed had these black, centipede-like insects burst open from their stomachs, metres in length and coiling around their bodies. Their sight truly wrenched Jack's guts through the cold shock. The insects were then cut out and removed by automatons that were looking after the process. From his drifting eyes, looking upon the spectre of this laboratory, barely even comprehending the actions which were taking place, he saw these same automatons collecting eggs which were lying at the bottom of many of the tanks as blood lingered around the female victims.

"What is this?"

"This is where the angels are made!"

Jack walked up to Dillion and slapped him the hardest he'd ever slapped anyone in his life. Dillion began crying in earnest, but a slap wasn't enough. Now that the shock was wearing off, and the anger dwindling, all that remained was bitter sadness and disappointment. Jack clenched his fists, planted one of his feet, and then shot an uppercut into Dillion's diaphragm. Dillion was launched into the air, as spittle flew from his mouth and his eyes widened in shock. Jack was vaguely aware of the gun brushing against his hand from the inside of his coat, but it wouldn't do, not until he beat this collective ugliness of human nature out of this man.

Dillion scrambled on the floor, frantically trying to make his distance from Jack. His feet slipped and his nails screeched against the polished tiles as he panicked. Jack wiped a tear away with a balled-up fist, and was about to grab onto Dillion's shirt by the neck, when he felt a streak of numbness connect across the left side of his face, as if he had been whipped.

He stumbled back, feeling his nose, only to see that Dillion was airborne. Tendrils of ripples hoisted him up, and coiling around him in protection. What sort of power is this? thought Jack. Dillion was still cringing with his arms over his face, which meant that it wasn't his own will which protected him, but something predominantly instinctual. He seemed too afraid and frail to retaliate by himself.

Whatever, I have to now, Jack thought, pulling his gun out in one swift motion, and firing mercilessly one shot after another towards Dillion, not betting his chances that only a couple of bullets would do their job. But the tendrils sprang forward with a speed quicker than bullets, creating cracks of thunder in the air. They absorbed all the bullets and hurled them back, penetrating Jack in his left thigh.

Jack flinched, never having had this much pain in a momentary flash. Somehow, the tendrils gently landed Dillion back onto the floor, and he took off. Jack followed, feeling the desperation of losing something which had been almost caught in the wind. The bullet in his leg made running unbearable, with shock passing through with each step. He stumbled once or twice, feeling a sudden adrenaline rush preventing him from falling over. But quick as he tried, Dillion turned left and disappeared into one of the sub-laboratories. The door immediately shut itself, which was an impenetrable steel bulwark.

Jack stood there, perplexed and confused, first breathing heavily, then letting the frustration consume him. He screamed until he was calmed, but the voice did not echo. He suddenly swung around, alarmed, realising that he'd been ambushed by the sound-devouring sycophants.

Before he could react, he felt red-hot coils of pain envelop his body from the waist to the neck as dark, unforgiving tentacles snatched him off the ground, digging into his skin with a tenacious grip. The antennae on these sycophants were like whips made for combat, and their bodies weren't shrivelled, gaunt and pale, but rather solid and menacing.

Suddenly, to his right, he noticed another sycophant holding onto someone, but he did not know who it was. It was a feminine figure… it was Reyn. Her eyes had gone pale and lifeless, and black veins webbed all over her torso. Something turned inside him when he saw her body turning grey by the second.

With a sound of metal sliding, the steel bulwark opened and Dillion stepped out. "This is what I wanted to show you," he said, waiting for a response. There was none. He scratched his chin, before his eyes lit up and he understood the purpose of the silence. "Oh no, you, it is her, I promise! I've rarely seen a specimen this impressive," he said, looking at her with an earnest smile of twisted admiration.

Jack felt a pang in his heart. He clenched his teeth, trying to grunt out his statement. "Don't look at her…"

"Why not? Do you not appreciate miracles?" he asked, underwhelmed at the reaction. "Ah, I will explain. Sycophants are a very unruly bunch. If I could turn her into the queen, it would finally solve the puzzle!" He spoke excitedly, as if he really wanted Jack to appreciate.

Jack couldn't scream. His lungs and his neck were compressed so tight that he couldn't even feel his throat vibrate. There were needles piercing his heart with each beat. Tch. Useless, so useless. His vision was blurring, and he was sure he was dying. Whatever. The pain didn't exist. Only his vision did, viewing the scene from a distant plane. Through his peripheral vision he saw Reyn's silhouette. There were multiple holes at her waist the size of a penny, where she must have been injected. There was another one on the left of her chest, above where her heart would be.

"All that remains is an injection through the head..." he heard the distant monster's whisper. "Easy now, children..." the man scoffed at his insect-like underlings. "Weaken your tenacity over them."

Jack was dragged back from his dream-like state, being able to breathe again. He grunted, and was surprised to hear the noise. The tentacle was loose enough for him to speak. He darted his gaze around the lab, looking for a way to escape this mess. What could he do? At last, a socket. There was a large, busted-up industrial socket on the wall in front of them. If only he could somehow shove the creature's antennae inside it. It was a considerable gamble, but he had to do it. His arms were bound, but he found enough room with his hands and leveraged the space to grab a handful of the long, tentacle-like antennae, and pulled it hard. The sycophant screeched as the pain shot up its eye socket.

Now! he thought to himself, and with a burst of raw energy, pulled his arms out of the coil as the sycophant became distracted by the pain. What an irony, he thought: its strongest part was attached to one of the most sensitive spots of the human anatomy. With his newfound freedom to move his arms, he twisted backwards to face the creature, grabbed onto both of the antennae near the eye sockets, and then pulled. The sycophant screeched, like a single locust lynched from the swarm.

It stumbled and fell backwards, letting go of Jack completely. Jack got up, quickly catching the tip of the antennae, and shoved it into the socket, praying for any nylon in his coat and the rubber in his shoes to protect him. The stars went through his eyes, and his body became momentarily numb as he landed on his butt. The sycophant had been electrocuted, killing it almost instantly.

All of this happened way too fast for someone like Dillion to react. Even now he seemed shocked, his eyes wide and mouth finding words to command the rather dull and confused sycophant still holding on to Reyn. Jack quickly dug in his pocket, found a throwing knife, and threw it at the other sycophant, nailing it in the head and killing it. It dropped to the floor, taking Reyn with it, as the antennae lost their strength and slowly let go of her.

Jack glared at Dillion, who jumped back in fear. Knowing Dillion's power, Jack doubted he'd be much of a nuisance if he avoided him. He rushed towards Reyn, hoping to God that he was correct that Dillion's power was only instinctual. Dillion leapt back fearfully, and tripped on the pipelines running through the lab. Jack quickly took the opportunity, hoisted Reyn up, and ran.

She really is heavy, he thought, being slower than anticipated with a shot leg. The man was up on his feet and chasing them in no time. Jack really tried to increase his pace, but the blood making it slippery didn't help, either.

My God, this one time I get the chance to save **you** and it has to be this nightmarish human factory, chased by a man child. It's like being thrown into a game at the hardest level.

Suddenly, he buckled to his knees and thought it was all over; but it wasn't true. It was the floor which had shook and his elbows had hit the floor, shooting up the most visceral of pain in his arms. But despite that, he did not let her hit the ground, not even her head, which was lolling from her being unconscious.

Somehow, Van Vuren and Maverick had broken through, along with some cavalry. The divine intervention had happened. They were battling sycophants, doing their best to cleave them before they vomited up their acid-spitting pipes.

Jack sighed, letting Reyn gently rest on the floor. Guilt immediately overtook him, for having all the harm come down her way. For all the times she had looked out for him, he had given no thought to her, the same way he had given no thought to Alex. Did he truly not realise the worth of what he was given until he had lost it?

More sycophants ran through the main entrance which Jack had left open. He had run up too close to the entrance to escape. The sycophants had already vomited up their acidic pipes and were ready to spray, so escape was not an option. He heaved her up and turned around. If they spat at him, then he'd be the one taking the hits. For the first time, he felt as if he was protecting someone else. For the first time, he had chosen someone else.

He shut his eyes and waited, and waited; but it did not happen. He finally dared to look up. Dillion had gotten up from the rubble which had taken him down with the explosion. He had called them off. "I do not want to kill you. You're the only one I've ever known with a remotely similar affliction to mine."

Jack just felt his mouth open and scream in panic. Van Vuren had heard him, and with great horror on his face, his eyes fell on Dillion. He knew him. They had met each other. One look was all it took for Jack to know. Dillion tried to speak again, but his forehead was pierced open, as Van Vuren did not take a moment to put an end to him with a bullet.

Reyn sprang to life, gasping for air. Her lifeless eyes now had their pupils returning, and the grotesque, black veins began to disappear. For a moment her eyes flitted across the room in terror, but then landed upon Jack's face, smeared by her blood, and then they immediately lost their hostility and fear.

"Reyn…" whispered Jack; but Reyn put her arm around him and pulled him in.

"Reyn... I am in..." a muffled voice said, as she held him by her chest.

"I don't care," she replied in a voice as her usual self. No matter what had happened after getting lost in the last few hours, it definitely felt pleasant being alive once again.

Respite

Jack helped Reyn to her feet. She seemed shaky, and unsure of her footing. Nevertheless, she asked him to unhand her, but ultimately lost balance the moment she was left alone, falling sideways until Jack caught her again.

"I am sorry. Looks like this time, I will have to…"

Reyn mustered a half smile endearingly. "You finally have your chance. Thanks for everything."

"Ah, whatever; the best a handicapped man can do in a race full of horses," he replied, placing her arm over his shoulder and securing her by the waist.

"Jack!" they heard Ashley cry as she frantically rushed towards them, followed closely by Lappy. "You okay?" she asked, with her eyes flitting indecisively between Jack and Reyn, unable to decide which one looked the worse. Reyn seemed the obvious choice, despite Jack's blood-soaked clothes and a pool forming by his feet.

"Reyn…" she whispered.

"I am fine," Reyn replied, with some strength returning to her voice.

"What happened?" asked Lappy in a shrivelled, terror-stricken tone.

"Not now." Jack frowned, indicating that both Ashley and Lappy stow away their inquiries for the moment. "We need to get Reyn out. Get her back to *NightScythe* and plug her on the life-support or whatever."

"Not going to be possible," Lappy said coldly. "We had a battle with a couple of Guren and some knights who had somehow caught the wind. One of our ships is gone, but anyway it's too risky to go back to the citadel's surface again. It is nearly three in the night, soon it will be dawn and the lack of the two Guren not reporting back and some missing knights means that it will be alarming enough for the Sanctum to take some serious action."

"What do we do, then?"

"Just let me heal her," Ashley butted in between the two. "Get her behind that piece of machinery there; I will heal her with as much strength as I've left. Just defend us from the sycophants."

And that was it. Despite Reyn's insistence, they left them behind the machinery and went to join the battle. Lappy took his discharge gun and went far right to Jack, hiding behind the tanks, luring and shooting sycophants once they had reached him. Jack had picked up his own gun which he had originally dropped nearby.

Now that he could see a view of the battle, he felt chills run up his spine. This was it, the final moment.

Within this lab, within the bowels of the citadel, the fate of mankind was going to be decided.

From this distance, he realised there were about fifty soldiers. They had arrived with a hundred and fifty, and about a third of them were present here. The sycophants were going down quick enough… but what was next? Was the secret to the aethernet and the Common Registry stored in this super-computer? Would it be all over if they could somehow disable the network with it?

Somehow it seemed possible; they had three hours until dawn, and all they had to do was to kill these sycophants, disable the system, and run as far as possible. Maybe to Scythe, where they'd all be safe; but it would still be the end of the Dark, the end of the last remaining organisation of a hundred thousand people being the hope of Sancta America. The continent would be lost to darkness, but they'd at least be able to broadcast the truth to the world.

With sudden goose-bumps at the end of his momentary introspection, he turned away from the fight happening at the far end of the lab and faced towards the row of screens attached to the row of monitors connected to the super-computer in front of him.

"Lappy!" he called boldly, who almost jumped back in surprise from the tension.

"You can feel it, too, Jack?" Lappy replied, answering the call.

Jack nodded. "The end is indeed near. Come quick, you always wanted to stand out and be something special. right? Do something with this super-computer, and use the aethernet to broadcast the truth in the minds of people across the world."

Lappy nodded and turned around, now walking parallel to Jack as they approached the computer. Jack felt his palms go cold and his nerves wracking, yet he simply smiled reassuringly to himself. They were three steps in now.

"ALL MEMBERS, HALLLLLT!" thundered a booming voice, so sudden that Jack almost felt his soul leave his body. He immediately swung back. It was Van Vuren, who within moments had spun twice and blown away a bunch of sycophants as quick as he could. The flow of them had ebbed for a moment, but that wasn't the worry.

"He's coming!" The foreboding words echoed through the lab.

Jack felt his blood drain away, and possibly everyone else's, too, within that moment. That was one statement they did not expect; or rather they prayed that they would not even have to expect.

The silence was deathly prevalent for a moment, before a couple of voices broke out. "What do we do, then?"

"Our power sensors are burnt out, meaning his private ship could be approaching. The ship might also have the Holy Knights in it..." said Van Vuren in his most collected voice, but for the first time, it was taut. Even to Jack, the tension was palpable. If Van Vuren was truly terrified… then Jack wouldn't want to know what awaited them. "Brandon, lead all the soldiers over there and meet the challenge on the surface. I will use the distraction to get the children out of the citadel and send them off on the ship."

Jack did not expect to hear this statement. Every soldier in the room nodded, as if somehow it made any sense. It did not. It was suicide they were going for.

"WE WILL NOT!" Jack heard Ashley scream, as she ran out from behind the machinery and suddenly burst into uncontrollable fits of tears, unable to utter anything else.

"I… I agree with her. Surely you all understand that this is…" said Jack, trying to support her.

"We don't have time," replied Van curtly, but not without his voice flinching.

"We don't have a family to turn back to…" said one man's voice from many of the people.

"Don't cry, this the first time we're ever gonna feel useful as the Dark's military anyway…" followed a woman's voice.

More voices went up, with each of them speaking, until finally what one man said, exhausted and emotionally devoid, stood out from the echo and struck Jack to his core: "We are all old here, and whoever of us had children… we've all lost them. Safe for you few, who I guess God left the Dark's future to be. If you can run away safely today, remember, nothing is on you. We chose this path, the path of revenge; the rest is up to you. The Dark will never die, as long as you, our children, live."

For a moment a profound silence followed, save for the beeping of the odd machinery. Jack had nothing to respond, but clench his fists and look at Ashley, who was still barely holding herself from falling over. He walked up to her and hugged her. Lappy ran towards them. They all walked over to Reyn and hoisted her up. Around the corner from the machinery appeared Maverick, who was fighting at the far end of the lab and was too guilt-stricken to speak.

They were all five together, and suddenly Jack realised the harrowing lack of Kiara there, of the twins Zachary and Ferrell. None of this would have happened if not for you...; he thought of Zach's face when he had said that to him. And suddenly, Jack felt his throat tighten up, and bitterness seeping into his mouth.

"Brandon, lead the charge," he heard Van call out, as the soldiers reassembled themselves in files and walked past them, following Master Brandon.

Jack only stared at the floor when everyone walked past, letting his steps lead him wherever the rest of the four went. Van Vuren did not wait for them all to leave; so, as soon as the five of them walked up to him, he picked up his pace, gesturing them to follow. Reyn's life somehow had recovered the moment Dillion was killed, so her power had gradually returned. It instinctively took her feet off the ground, cushioning her in the air, so that her body wouldn't have to experience the pain. It also made it a tad easier for them to drag her, as Van led them through the tunnels torn open by the earlier explosions.

The gospel of a new day

Brandon stood at the surface level of the citadel. The Dark's device was beeping with a steady rhythm, but the ship hadn't appeared yet. It must be in some close proximity. Upon reaching the surface, he'd ordered the soldiers in groups to be positioned across at various points. His strategy was going to have them hide and sabotage the ship by firing at it collectively before it could land.

Time ticked and the device beeped, but he felt an overwhelming sense of confidence welling within, mixed with satisfaction and a tinge of sadness. His feelings were quite a contrast to their final, deterministic moment. But it was as if, upon the dawn of his final time ticking, something that he'd felt devoid of all his life had been fulfilled. And he realised that beyond the edges of the citadel in the sky, it was a clear and beautiful sky; blue as the ocean, and the clouds were white and sinless.

Gazing at the mountains painted rich green with forests and stretching across the canvas of the horizon… a memory came back in the form of realisation. The edge of the citadel was like a fenceless narrow road slithering up a perilous mountain, where he'd once been, sitting as a child in the car. Back then, it was terrifying, but he trusted his father. His life was in the palm of his father's hand that controlled the wheel. And that, at the time, soothed him... it was okay to be in the back seat and let someone else decide the currents of his life.

Time went on and he grew up; being an honour graduate of the Dark's military school, his father's job naturally fell into his lap. He did as he was instructed, teaching the children as he was supposed to. He'd developed a rapport with them, as upon passing to the next grade and growing up, they would always remember Brandon from all the masters. Brandon, the friendliest and the least scornful master, they would say. Brandon, the nicest fellow the other masters would say. The capable and the deserving fellow military commanders would say.

He was nothing short of well-loved. But nothing he did was loved because he did something special. All he had to offer was niceness. And that he did, for lack of other interests or the power to take control of the wheel of his life. Perhaps it wasn't just only as a child when he decided to kick back and allow his life take its course, but rather the road where he gave up his fate to someone else, still kept going until today.

He had nothing to offer, but he did not regret it. The only conflict was a little void within, never being filled up. Maybe it was that being a master and having nothing of essence which he could pass on to his students left him unsatisfied. Maybe giving them something of a purpose, he thought, would mean more than being generous. But that only reminded him, how could he do that… when he was just a child himself taken by where the wheel carried him?

What was I there for? What was it that I had to show? he thought. This time, however, in his final and rarest instance, he was finally forced to take the wheel.

"Brandon!" a voice called from the back seat of the car.

Who… a student of mine? Just when I took my first wheel, I wished to have you see it. Now you can see me… finally doing it. The view is beautiful, my child. I understand now, I always meant to show you this view.

"BRANDON!" a voice called again. It was Karyn stepping in, dressed in the same deep green Dark military uniform that she wore back in the day as his student, except it was for a real, life-threatening situation this time. Her tousled red hair fell to her shoulders in a familiar sight. But the girl known to be cool and ambitious, with a confident smile, had her eyes wide open and glaring at him.

He snapped back, looking at her unhinged state, "Yes, Karyn?"

"What are you looking at?"

"At the horizon for the approaching ship."

"No, I mean what the heck are you looking at as the commander? Don't you see we're all like fucking dead bodies abusing our boundaries? We shouldn't even be standing here walking like this."

"What do you mean? Karyn, is this not an honour? A day we looked forward to…"

"SCREW THAT! What honour is in this…? Brandon, you remember that… the Dark is gone?" she said with delirious eyes and quivering lips, until they broke into a nervous smile; the smile of a forlorn gaze lost in a distant memory. "You know I saw the kids from the primary running on and about the grass. That little Jason was there, wearing blue overalls and all. Then they were falling like flies. And off into the distance, the city was falling, burning away, and nothing but smoke reached up to the ceiling."

Brandon felt his jaw drop. Surely… she hadn't just broken under the trauma?

"The morning is over, Brandon! The morning where we were all going to business. What remain are us, some dead bodies trampling over that beautiful morning!"

Brandon twitched. He didn't know how to respond… he had the wheel, but this passenger in the back seemed unhappy. Karyn smiled for a few more moments, her glossy eyes still gazing off into the distant memory. But, eventually, she shook her head and turned on her heel, walking away unsteadily. I can't just let that happen, he thought.

"Karyn, wait! Stop, what are you going to do…?" he said, as he reached for her and grabbed her by the wrist.

"I mean, if we're going to die burning from that ship, we might as well walk off the edge!"

"Karyn… don't tell me you hate the kids for us being in this position?"

She turned back with her eyes still in a delirious glare, but tears were running down her face. "Of course not, Brandon. I am glad they are escaping; at least they will live to find some other morning again…"

She became momentarily silent, but her face kept smiling. "But for me, I am going home, I miss my family…" she said, as with her other hand she pulled her gun out, and the bullet went through her temple before Brandon could even register it. The sadness left her eyes, leaving only opaque marbles, and the conflicted smile remained only of a mannequin frozen in time.

As her corpse fell onto the ground, her hand remained in Brandon's. She left the back seat just when I was about to drive the car… is there no one who wants to see me drive it?

"Captain Brandon!" someone called out with a grim expression and a dour look on their face. All the members from their positions were looking at him for something… something? Oh. The ship had appeared into clear view, heading for the citadel grounds, engulfed by a shield of flame. It intended to scorch everything on the surface as it landed.

So be it… I have this car and I have just realised, it was always heading towards the edge, he thought, as a part of him screamed some brief command, and all the members charged towards the centre of the ground, ready to shoot at the ship with all their force.

I will drive you safely to the beautiful forest over the edge, just hold on. My Children.

Light

They were about to emerge from one of the cave systems exits. Parallel to them was the final cave wall, and not too far ahead of them was the exit hewn through it. The bright sunlight spilled from the hole and tinted the floor with a warm yellowish hue. It was like a promise after hours of bleakness.

However, the air of tension lingered, taut as a bowstring. Mere moments ago, there had been an impact on the surface, shaking them all the way into the bowels of the citadel. It was hard to know whether the ship had been taken down or something truly foreboding had transpired. But one thing which terrified Jack the most was that Van Vuren's device had stopped beeping. It could mean that the ship was gone for good… but wasn't it Paragon's own ship? What if Paragon himself had decided to step into the situation — in which case… what will we do?

As they ran, Van briefly glanced back and exclaimed in his most urgent tone, "The *NightScythe* is hovering right beneath the exit, so as soon as you reach — jump and you will fall through the ship's roof hatch. Do not waste your time thinking."

The tension in his voice was beyond breaking point… or, for the first time, was it fear which Jack was sensing? Is Van scared for the same reason I am? If so… these last dozen metres feel like infinity. As they approached the final distance, there was a moment of prominent and serene silence permeating the atmosphere with the steady thumps of their footsteps. The red glow of the breaking dawn fell over his face as they reached towards the light. It was a trance-like sensation felt after a peaceful sleep. This was one of those times where he felt such sensation welling deep within his bowels, but… what could it mean? What do such feelings even mean when it comes down to it?

The ground shook, the earth split, and he briefly remembered the darkness burying the light as dust came to life and blurred everything in sight. While he scrambled to rub the dust off his eyes, he heard the confused whispers of reception all around him, the whispers which addressed the figure none other than him.

"My apologies for the abrupt entrance; the ship could not sustain the landing," a soothing, polite voice responded to the confused whispers. Jack could still only see the silhouette of the man through the amalgam of lingering dust and the light flooding through the hole, and although he still did not know who this man was, he heard Van Vuren speak.

"Beck," whispered Van Vuren; a name that Jack did not expect to hear.

WHAT? What in the living hell? His reality spun, ceasing to make sense. As the dust finally settled, he saw the familiar face with slicked brown hair streaked with a patch of white. Jack could only gape in utter astonishment. "Mr… Beck?" From the office? Him? What the…?

"Then the soldiers I left outside…?" The terror dawned upon Van's face as he realised the precedent.

"My condolences," Mr Beck replied.

It shot chills through Jack's spine. It was true then? No, it was an undeniable reality that this divine voice, and the angelic kindness of face, was none other than of that man. How could anyone but him be the Paragon? His sheer aura buzzed Jack to his core. And when Mr Beck finally opened his eyes, the deep colour of honey, mixed with the yellowish tint of the sunlight spilling across his face, made Jack forget everything. It was Mr Beck in his true form, in his true divine light.

"What are you here for, Beck…? Why did you do this?" Van Vuren trembled with the most visceral fury Jack had ever seen anyone in. But the way he addressed Beck, it was as if this wasn't the first time he had encountered him. There had been a history between these men before.

"You know why I had to. The amnesty had to be broken." He then looked towards them, especially at Jack. "I am sorry. It seems that, for the sake of peace,

Van Vuren has kept the truth of the second century war hidden," he said. "It was all due to Van Vuren's effort that the Dark enjoyed peace. Two hundred years ago, he bent the knee during our fourth battle, and as such, a truce was formed. Now I know that the citizens of Dark would rather die than forfeit, and you were told that the battle was fought bravely and you were crushed with your honour intact... Well, that wasn't the case. Peace was bought for pride, some allies on your side betrayed; some other factions of the Dark who disagreed with the treaty were sentenced. How you take this knowledge... is up to you, but for me it is honourable for a man to betray his ideals for the prosperity of greater good. What he did back then was certainly undeserving of scorn."

"You dishonourable old fool!" Maverick bawled, rushing over to Van Vuren and jerking him by the collar. Van Vuren did little to resist.

"Calm down, Maverick, he did what had to be done," Reyn painfully told him, as she dragged him back.

Now that Maverick was off him, Van turned his attention fully to Beck. "But why, Beck? WHY? Why would you go to such twisted lengths to break the amnesty? I cannot believe that I kept my faith in your words and held back, despite all the strange occurrences starting from the reappearance of these two."

And then Jack saw it. For the first time in this encounter, there was a tinge of apprehension on Beck's face, almost as if he was bearing a truth which no one quite understood. "No, Van... the rift is widening." Beck then turned to face the sky through the hole he'd created. "I had to. Your people grew so many and so quick in numbers that the heart of the rift in Scythe was being pulled open like a cloth torn apart by being pulled onto its ends." He then turned towards Jack and Maverick, with a look of genuine pity. "You... were the reaper's sickle, and you the scythe. You were arrested and thrown into Raellslov prison along with Grim as per the terms of the amnesty at the end of the war. We wiped your memories out long ago. We only released you again with false memories, false friends, and false experiences so we could lure the Dark out. Allen's murder and overseeing you were a part of it. Fred was someone which the Dark trusted, and we had convinced him to our cause when he himself showed up to ask for our help. The Scythe is being overrun by inexplicable horrors with the widening of the rift, opening up the astral dimension, and there was no other way to save this planet besides doing what I just did."

No one spoke or made a sound. They had all bought into Fred's trickery until the bitter end. It did not even come as a shock with the events in mind. Jack was shaking, not because he was angry, but because the truth scared him. His greatest fear was always losing his identity, only to be told that he... he was someone else. Alex... his family, Allen... even the Arch-knight — all were the victims of his plot.

From a distance, he heard Van Vuren speak. "And what evidence do you have? Or is it just another excuse for your hollow ego? Hollow as the false idol of worship which you've become?"

Beck briefly turned back to face them with a glimpse of genuine anguish in his eyes, before he turned his back on them completely and said, "My truth lies in the fact that I do not justify it."

Sighing audibly, he regained his composure and called to no one in particular, as if addressing someone behind a fallen part of the wall, "Well, then, it seems I must call the ships to escort these two."

"I have contacted the ships, although this really hurts still," said Dillion, as he walked out, his clothes still visibly blood-soaked, and there was a scar on his head where the bullet hole was supposed to be.

Jack felt nothing but cold frustration, even more so than shock. It all made sense; if only he had seen the strings, he would not have walked into the web. But Maverick wasn't done speaking. "I have nothing at all to say to this pathetic old man here. But you, how can you speak of good? How can you pretend you even have good intentions?"

The ground shook, and Jack remotely remembered being enveloped by Reyn's sphere, as the ceiling broke, boulders crashed onto the ground, and similarly rock split from the earth and shot upwards. It was like a massive surge of power which he had never felt before. Maverick screamed, followed by a direct charge at Paragon. He was going in for the kill. Despite being wrapped in the bubble, the surge of power releasing from Maverick was so strong that even Reyn's diamond-like shield was shattering.

Surely, it was going to be the end of all of them there. But as sudden as his fit of rage was, it instantly stopped. The dust was settled, the roof thatched up, the ground stopped moving. Beck stood there, wiping the sleeve of his brown blazer. At his feet was Maverick, unconscious and vomiting onto the floor. It was like he was dead. But Beck placed a foot on him and he sprang to life, gasping for breath. Just what is this man? Who will overpower...? No, we cannot even comprehend him.

Beck had a very agitated look to him as he stared down on Maverick with a mix of pity and disdain. "Look, look into this world very carefully. The world is free. Free from the shadows of our fathers. Free from their divisions complicating the truth that we were but one species, gestated and nurtured by the same mother that is earth. And yet, they were different; they believed in ancient tales, and swore by it. Their borders, their differences, all were a deep gash holding them from the true enlightenment — an enlightenment that we'd be much better off as a species if all such divisions ceased to exist. And I have done that, even if it may be me who bears the gravest sin for it. The Paragon is just a symbol to unify them; it has nothing to do with my own pleasure."

"Beck." It was Van Vuren who spoke this time. He had a trigger in his hand. "Do not assume that you have us subdued. I planted a bomb in your laboratory before we left. Farewell to your satellite and aethernet system. I bid you good luck controlling the people in the mass confusion. Prepare yourself — this time the war will not end." And with that, he pressed the button. The whole citadel shook, and one last thing Jack remembered was the pure white canvas overtaking his vision.

Raellslov

Jack and Maverick were walking along the bleached-white tiles of a narrow corridor of a prison. A prison hidden behind walls as thick as ancient tree trunks and gated by metal doors so dense, it made bank vaults seem fragile. Escorting them were two tall and white automated droids, with two small green lights for their eyes.

As they walked, their handcuffs and fetters clicked sombrely in an otherwise stern silence. Both on their wrists and ankles, the cuffs were designed in such an eccentric way, it was almost as if they were a fashion statement, but there seemed to be more to them.

They were of a specific design made of silver, and on their wrist was a thin, silver clasp, like a curved bracelet, which dug into their skin and locked their wrists. And welded to each of the clasps through tiny spokes was a bigger shackle surrounding the clasp like the outside of a wheel, which was too big for their hands, but it was engraved with gold symbols. It looked ceremonial at first, but then Jack realised that they might actually have been runes; the runes which restricted power. So it's like a handcuff over a handcuff, huh? One which is a good old physical restriction and the fancy one attached to it as the means of restraining the power?

Every five metres or so apart, along the length of the hall, were the doors of each of the subsequent cells. They seemed tough, but not as impregnable as the main vaulted entrance. Guess they didn't have to be, when the inmates were so silent and subdued that the facility seemed eerily dilapidated. It was strange for him, because when he previously thought of Raellslov, the prison for the vilest criminals on the planet, he imagined it to have a raucous, menacing, and cut-throat environment. But here, the silence wasn't imposing, like that which is barely maintained by heavy security, but rather that it felt genuine and eerie.

For each of these cells, there were tiny viewing windows on the uppermost part of the gates. When he tried to look through them as they walked by, he noticed that the inmates were eerily slumped on their benches against the wall. Sometimes they'd be slouched on the floor or their chairs directly facing the window and staring through them as they walked by. Their eyes seemed pale and glassy. Even their bodies seemed paled, languid, and, more importantly, almost still. He couldn't stare back at them; they were all slumped in unnatural positions. It was as if they were dead, but barely kept alive.

Maverick might have noticed the same, too. "I can't feel my power," he said, shaking his shackles.

"Seems like this place restricts power, then." Jack was beyond sure that it was actually true.

"Well, then... did you see those guys...? Whatever it is doing to them, it really isn't healthy."

Jack nodded. If this place had kept them looking like they were twenty for the past hundred and seventy years or so after the war, then it was far from a normal place. He could feel Maverick shudder. He'd be afraid, too, had he power which he could lose. But he was feeling the opposite: instead of the cold shackles pressing onto his skin and reminding him of how painfully normal and un-powered his hands were, he felt a distant buzzing through them. Maybe it was just placebo, which he was more inclined to believe, but something about this prison was eerily familiar... what even went down here the last time?

The only answer to his thoughts were Maverick's buried whimpering as one of the droids held him by the arm and led him off into one of the intersecting corridors. Jack was truly alone now, just the way he started from his office apartment. Moments went by, and before he knew it, he was introduced to his cell. This one seemed to be somewhere at the end of the facility.

The droid stopped, and the gate was open before he knew it. Jack's cell was a ten by five feet, miserable, rectangular, white-washed hell with a fairly low ceiling. When the door closed, the bright lights he saw from the outside instantly disappeared. It was darkness, except for the light coming from the viewing window. But he couldn't look outside through it; it was just a white, undefined and impenetrable light.

So that's how it is, huh…? But in those purest moments of isolation, he felt something like a draught, like a trickle of ripples seeping from the crack under the door. As his eyes were closed, he felt as though the same cold draught was trying to reach his mind. "Whoever it is, I don't care anymore, so you might as well come in…"

The thought was met, and in a gruff yet kindly voice taking shape in his head, he was told, "I am glad to see you're still alive, Jack. I am Grim, one of the four horsemen of the apocalypse and a founder of the city of Dark. It is time that we meet again."

Prologue

The aroma of the woodland flushed her nostrils. Right over this rolling hill the gigantic forest of Scythe would begin, where they could hopefully meet the other camps.

The fresh, stark scent of the pine cones and the sugary hint of the tree saps, the earthly smell of soil and the petrichor spread into the air after the morning drizzle welcomed her. It was a scent of her childhood from a distant spring.

It took days of continuous walking, and navigation over the Ural Mountains, which had finally gotten them there. At nights, she would get to experience sleeping by a campfire and a shelter beneath the tree branches. The air in the open would be refreshing, and seeing the direct moonlight over her would be an enchanting experience; but it was hard for her to catch up on her sleep. The first time I've seen the actual night; the first time I am not sleeping inside that cave, she thought each night.

Her eyes felt heavy and strained, but she was eager to see what this mystical forest would bring. Only if… she thought, glancing at the others walking beside her. Zack, Ferrell, Kiara… even Jack and

Maverick. All that remained now was Lappy, who'd gone mute, with his torn, blue windbreaker and tattered jeans, and Ashley, with her tattered, white, oversized T-shirt soaked with bloody red scratches sustained through the journey. Van Vuren led them all this time, but he hadn't really talked or looked back at them since forever.

Before she knew it, the sight of the forest finally broke into view. It was dense, lush and alive. The conifers at the foremost lines welcomed them, their branches dancing in the morning wind. The soaring cedars shimmied and the strangler figs beautifully draped their vines over the host trees. The floor was covered by roots, bushes, leaves and wet mud. In the morning drizzle, everything looked glistening and new.

Despite everything that has happened…

The morning sunshine broke through the canopy and spilled its lukewarm light across the landscape, making its way through the chill air which previously pierced her to the bones. It warmed her skin, but also her soul, with its soft glow.

Despite being dealt such a cruel fate…

The animals which she had never seen before or were presumed extinct, or some entirely new species, appeared in her sight the more she looked. Little light blue monkeys the size of small birds perched upon the tree branches like tiny Christmas ornaments. They were in little families, with babies clinging to their mothers and small enough to fit in her palm. A bird nearly three metres tall like a giant cassowary but with lilac plumage and a crown made of yellow, red and blue feathers sang a beautiful song, facing towards the sky. There were even multiple tiger-like cats, but the size of a plump, orange tabby. Critters like squirrels, rats and echidnas scuffled through leaves and scuttled up and down the trees.

Even after existing a life which did not matter…

It is strange that…

Van Vuren stopped, pitching a foot on a rock and scanning the forest with his binoculars. He turned around, for the first time in three days, and despite his reddened and sunken eyes, he was smiling. "It is strange that the world still lives on."